"I asked if yo

Gideon scratched the stubble at his jaw. He had to stop staring at the woman. He'd scare her to death if he didn't act more like a gentleman. "I'd love a piece of your pie."

He followed her through the living room and into the kitchen. She turned around and almost ran into him. Almost, but not quite. He would have loved a reason to wrap his arms around her for a second.

She motioned toward the table. "My mom's asleep in the spare bedroom upstairs. She's spending the weekend with me."

"That's nice." By the pained expression that wrapped her face, Gideon wondered if it wasn't such a nice thing.

Lydia laid the plate of pie on the table. It smelled good, and he wondered where she'd bought it. He took a bite. "This is terrific." He jammed his fork back into the piece and shoveled pie into his mouth. "Where did you get this?"

"I told you I made it."

"When?"

"Out on the porch."

When I started daydreaming about freckles, no doubt. "Well, this is really good."

A slight blush tinted her cheeks and her eyes smiled contentedly with her lips. "You're the second person to say that today. Thank you."

In all his twenty-eight years, Gideon had never felt such an urge to kiss a woman. He didn't know it was possible for a man to go "cuckoo," as he and his brothers used to tease their sisters. Somehow, this lady who couldn't keep track of her dog, whom he'd only met one time before, this woman, who'd captured his mother's heart, had also captured his.

He loved the idea of it.

JENNIFER JOHNSON and her unbelievably supportive husband, Albert, are happily married and raising Brooke, Hayley, and Allie, the three cutest young ladies on the planet. Besides being a middle-school teacher, Jennifer loves to read, write, and chauffeur her girls. She is a member of the American Christian Fiction Writers. Blessed beyond measure, Jennifer hopes to always think like a child—bigger than imaginable and with complete faith. Send her a note at jenwrites4god@bellsouth.net.

Books by Jennifer Johnson

HEARTSONG PRESENTS
HP725—By His Hand
HP738—Picket Fence Pursuit
HP766—Pursuing the Goal

In Pursuit of Peace

Jennifer Johnson

Heartsong Presents

This book is dedicated to my youngest daughter, Allie. Allie, I love your zest for life, your ability to make us smile, and that you are your own unique self. There is no one like Allie, and I praise God for you. Seek Him always!

Thank you Albert, Brooke, Hayley, and Allie, who have always been a tremendous support to me. Thank you Rose McCauley for being such a wonderful crit partner and JoAnne Simmons for being such a great editor. Most importantly, I praise You, Jesus. You give us dreams and then You fulfill them in the way that is best for Your glory. May I always live for You.

A note from the Author:
I love to hear from my readers! You may correspond with me by writing:

> **Jennifer Johnson**
> **Author Relations**
> **PO Box 721**
> **Uhrichsville, OH 44683**

ISBN 978-1-60260-046-1

IN PURSUIT OF PEACE

Scripture taken from the HOLY BIBLE, NEW INTERNATIONAL VERSION®. NIV®. Copyright © 1973, 1978, 1984 by International Bible Society. Used by permission of Zondervan. All rights reserved.

Our mission is to publish and distribute inspirational products offering exceptional value and biblical encouragement to the masses.

PRINTED IN THE U.S.A.

one

Peering from a second-story window, Lydia Hammond watched as the little critter's nose dug into the loosened soil of the newly planted bed of impatiens. Pink and white petals flew through the air like a fireworks explosion. The damage did not deter the critter as it plowed into the neighboring daylily whose bright yellow flowers had only just begun to open.

"That little rascal!" Using all the strength she could muster between her thumb and index finger, Lydia tried to pry open the window's lock. "Ugh." She pounded the glass when the lock wouldn't budge.

Her new puppy—the part lab, part beagle, part whatever that she'd felt sorry for because the most adorable boy Lydia had ever seen was giving puppies away at the local supermarket, and it happened to be the last one in the box, so she'd melted and taken the little ball of fur despite her better judgment—looked up at her. The puppy seemed to smile mischievously before plowing his face and front paws back into the broken leaves and mutilated petals.

She pounded again, but the animal simply dug with more tenacity, as if he knew his time was limited. And still his little bottom and tail, lifted high in the air, wagged with excitement, as if he'd found the greatest creation of God—dirt.

"George!" Lydia yelled as she raced down the stairs of her grandmother's Victorian home. Without taking the care it deserved, she flung open the heavy front door, one of the few original items her grandparents had been able to nurture back to life after they purchased the century-old house. Of course, her grandfather had passed away before Lydia was born, so she'd always considered the home her grandmother's. She pushed open the beveled-glass storm door designed specifically to complement the original door.

"George!" she yelled again, thinking for some odd reason how the name she'd given the critter really didn't fit him. He should be called "Scamp," or "Rascal," or "Nuisance." George really didn't even sound like a dog's name.

"Listen here, you little ragamuffin." She bent down to pick up the puppy. Instead, George lifted his dirt-covered nose from the soil and jumped toward her. Filthy paws painted her light khaki capris in various places. His tail wagged in utter delight as she twisted and turned, trying to grab the puppy without adding additional splotches to her clothing.

Finally getting hold of him around the belly, she scooped him into the crook of her arm but still tried to hold him away from her chest. "Look what you did." She pointed with her free hand toward the mess he'd created. She'd spent several hours that morning planting flowers the way she'd seen Grandma do it the four years Lydia lived with her during her parents' bitter divorce.

A shot of pain arrowed through her heart as Lydia thought of her earthly champion's death. Grandma had only been gone four months. Though Lydia hadn't lived with the older woman for five years, she still envisioned Grandma rocking on the front porch, standing in the kitchen pondering which dessert to bake, or hanging clothes on the clothesline as she did every summer because "windblown garments smelled better than dryer-dried clothes."

Lydia was thankful her mother and aunt were allowing her to stay in Grandma's house. She had been here three weeks. She needed a fresh start, and being near Grandma's memories seemed right. *Of course Mom would say I've had plenty of fresh starts.* And in truth, her mom was right. Lydia'd had more jobs in her twenty-four years than most people had in a lifetime.

Through high school, she'd worked at various fast-food restaurants, a grocery store, and even a video store. In college, she'd worked at an elementary school as a custodian, which meant she cleaned vomit-ridden floors, missed urinals, and worse. If she had her way, she'd never clean again. Yet because she loved getting to know the kids and their families, she decided to take a few education classes. That lasted a little over a semester.

A year later, Lydia landed a job at an art gallery. She loved meeting the interesting people who painted and sculpted. She found their passion contagious and decided to take a few art classes in college. That didn't even last a full semester.

She met a girl who got her hooked on aerobics, and she studied to be an aerobics instructor. Lasted a year.

She tried her hand at a bank job. She worked at a movie theater. And a dentist's office. She tried working with infants at a day care—definitely not her kind of job. After the first nasty diaper, Lydia hightailed it out of there.

Then she met a girl named Samantha Lily. Sam had a contentedness Lydia had never before witnessed, except in Grandma. When the job got hard, Sam stuck it out. When money became tight, Sam kept on going. When Lydia's grandma died, Sam proved to be a constant friend. When Lydia had questions about why Sam proved different, Sam told her about Jesus.

Lydia's life completely changed when she met Him.

She closed her eyes and muttered a quick prayer for Sam's protection. Lydia hadn't spoken with Sam since she began her position as a teacher in China. "May she lead many to You, Jesus."

A beep sounded from inside the house. She opened her eyes and gasped. "The pie! I'm glad I set the timer." Lydia looked down at her little varmint. "You're coming with me." George wagged his tail and licked her hand. A smile tugged at her lips. She couldn't deny she liked the little guy's never-ending enthusiasm.

Racing into the bathroom, she grabbed the hand towel from its hook. She held George over the tub with one hand and scrubbed his head and paws with the other.

Beeps continued to echo through the house, and Lydia's heart sped to match them. "I don't want that pie to ruin, but I don't want you to ruin any of Grandma's furniture either." The pup squirmed in her hand, and she released him when she felt confident he wouldn't make a bigger mess in the house.

She quickly washed her hands before rushing into the kitchen. After grabbing two pot holders off the countertop, she pulled open the oven door. The sweet aroma of cinnamon and apple filled the air. The lightly browned piecrust looked perfect as Lydia pulled her homemade dessert from the oven. "I think she'll like this. As soon as it's cool, I'll cut two generous pieces out of it."

Lydia glanced down at George, who'd joined her in the kitchen. His eyes seemed to beg for a taste as his wet nose sniffed the air. She bent down and scratched his head. "Pie is not for puppies, but hopefully Mrs. Andrews will like it."

Lydia thought of the older lady she had met at church

on Sunday. Mrs. Lorma Andrews had been the first one to greet Lydia. She'd even sat with her. The woman reminded Lydia so much of her grandmother that when she learned Mrs. Andrews lived only a mile away, Lydia knew she had to visit her.

"We're just going to walk right over there. The exercise will be good for both of us." She looked at George. "Maybe you'll want to take a nap when we get home."

Wishing she'd been able to use fresh apples to make the pie, Lydia'd had to settle for store-bought ones. Her grandma had an apple tree in the backyard, but it was still too early in the summer. Apples wouldn't be ready for picking until closer to fall. *Hopefully, it will still be good. Even Mom can't help but approve of my apple pies.*

She headed toward the stairs so she could run up to her room and change clothes. Her mother's approval had always been so important to her. For some reason, she wanted Mrs. Andrews to be pleased with her, as well.

&

Gideon Andrews gripped the last two buckets of peaches in his hands. Having decided to try something new, he'd sectioned out a few rows of orchard land to the west of his home and planted several Eldorado Miniature peach trees. The fifteen-acre apple orchard had been a lucrative purchase for him two years before. The previous owner, Gideon's agricultural mentor during his college years, decided to retire with his new wife and move to Florida, leaving an already established, well-known children's activity area filled with several pieces of playground equipment, an apple art activity area, and even a petting zoo. The transfer of ownership had been as smooth as a full-grown, fresh-picked apple.

Gideon gave the credit to God. His entire life had God's fingerprints all over it. He knew God, and God alone, had blessed him with the chance to purchase the orchard just four years out of college.

Old Amos, their local supermarket manager, had predicted the worst. *He won't make it six months.* The man had pounded his fist against a counter when Gideon's mentor had introduced him to Amos.

A smile lifted Gideon's lips. Now, Amos bought from Gideon before any of the other orchard owners. In fact, it was Amos who'd encouraged Gideon to try growing another fruit. "How 'bout some peaches?" The old man raised his eyebrows and winked. "I believe you could make you a good piece of money off peaches, as well."

And peach trees Gideon had planted. He figured it would be worth it to try his hand at an additional fruit. Having decided to start small at first, Gideon would plant more trees if the peaches sold well locally.

The weight of his load lightened as Gideon thought of the six filled buckets already sitting next to his back door. It was still early, the middle of June, and he'd been able to pick eight bucketfuls. He wouldn't sell these. Mama would enjoy canning some, and they could eat some fresh, as well. She could make a few pies, maybe some tarts. His mouth watered at the thought of Mama's homemade peach cobbler covered with vanilla ice cream.

Mama's moving in with him about a year ago, more than a year after his father's death, had been quite an adjustment. He wasn't used to having someone tell him to tuck in his shirt, wipe his shoes, and shave his stubble. In the past, he'd let his beard grow out the full week, waiting to shave before church on Sunday. Mama'd have none of that. "God gave you a nice face," she'd fuss, "and I want to see it." He shook his head. He wouldn't argue with clean clothes on his back, crisp sheets on his bed, and home-cooked meals filling his belly. No, the good definitely outweighed the bad.

His house came into view, and he noticed again that several of the roof's shingles seemed loose in the back. They'd had some good rain through May, and he'd neglected to check it out when he first noticed it. *This afternoon I'm going to take a look.*

He took another step and found his foot slipping. He flapped his arms to keep from falling backward. Peaches spilled from his buckets. "What in the world?"

Gaining his footing, he looked down and noted the partially smashed peach wearing his shoe print. "It must have fallen. . . ." He surveyed the yard splattered with peaches. "What happened—"

Before he could finish, a black-and-brown-speckled ball of fur tore around the corner of the house. Juice spilled from the peach the creature had clutched between its jaws. Upon seeing Gideon, the critter dropped the fruit and raced toward him. It yelped and wagged its tail while scratching at the bottom of his jeans.

"Where did you come from?" Gideon scooped up the animal and strode toward the house. The pup tried to lick his hand, and Gideon repositioned him. He was cute, but they did not need a dog. Gideon's ire rose as he walked past a dozen or more smashed peaches. *I'm glad Mama is here, but she cannot just decide to get a dog without at least talking with me about it.*

He passed more damaged fruit. *How am I supposed to tell if I want to plant more next year if I can't see if I like the fruit? I'm not selling something that isn't of good quality.* He passed the buckets; each lay toppled over.

"Look what you've done," he growled at the pup as he neared the back door. "Mama, we do not need a dog! You need to talk to me about these things!" He burst through the door. "Come out here and see what it's done. It's ruined—"

A young woman jumped up out of a chair. Her eyes, lighter than the sky above him, widened in surprise. She pushed long locks of reddish-blond curls behind her ear. "I'm sorry." She grabbed the pup from his hands. "George, what have you done now?" she whispered through gritted teeth.

Gideon glanced at his mom. Her lips lifted in a tight smile, but he knew she masked a scowl. Her hand firmly planted on her hip gave away her frustration. "Gideon, this is Lydia Hammond." Mama motioned toward the beauty, whose face had reddened to the point that her freckles had disappeared. "She's living in her grandmother's home. You remember Marian Smith?"

"Uh, sure." He glanced down at his feet and realized he'd tracked a bunch of dirt onto the floor. "I'm. . ."

"I'm sorry. I don't know how he got off the leash. I'll pick up the mess right now." Lydia opened the door.

"No. It's no big deal." His all-of-a-sudden parched mouth burned, and his throat closed, making it hard for him to swallow or speak. Clearing his throat, he willed his mouth to obey his need to speak. "I didn't mean to sound so abrupt."

"It's my fault." She raced out the door and started gathering peaches before he could say another word.

He turned to Mama, whose anger proved evident now. "We better go help." She started out the door.

Dumbfounded, he watched the two for a few seconds. He

was a heel. A big, overgrown heel. He always barked before he knew the facts. Now he'd embarrassed his mother and a woman—a rather attractive woman. He stepped out the door. "It's really not necessary."

"I think that's most of them." Lydia turned toward him, made eye contact for a moment, and then looked away. Red spread across her cheeks. "I'm sorry to meet you under these circumstances. I was really excited to see you." She sucked in her breath. "I mean. . .because Mrs. Andrews spoke so much of you. Not your looks per se." She flailed her free hand in front of her face. "I mean. . .she said you were nice looking." Her blush deepened. "Not that I care. I mean. . .I *care* because I like your mother. But looks don't matter. I mean. . .I guess they matter some." She smacked her thigh then waved slightly. "I'll just go now. Bye."

"What?" Gideon scratched the top of his head. Was the woman saying he was cute or ugly? Why would they talk about that anyway? He'd had enough matchmaking in his life. If Mama was considering setting him up, he'd have to let her know better. He turned toward Mama. Pinched lips, squinted eyes, and a snarl lifting one side of her nose told him that now was not the best time to discuss matchmaking. Feeling very much like a little boy again, he shrugged his shoulders. "Mama, I didn't know you had a guest."

"You embarrassed that poor child to death," Mama repri- manded. "She's new here and lonely. She's taken Marian's death hard, and her good, Christian neighbors should be there to lend her a helping hand."

Gideon smacked his hands to his sides. He'd never meant to hurt the woman. He would never intentionally hurt anyone, not even the little pup that ruined six buckets of peaches. "I'm sorry."

"I think you'll have to tell Lydia that."

Gideon blew out a long breath. He glanced toward Lydia. She'd already made it a good distance from his house.

"What's wrong, Gideon?" His mother's tone had changed to concern. "You're not usually that quick to anger."

"Nothing really." The day started to press down on his heart at his mother's innocent question. If she pried, he feared more emotion than he cared to display would spill from within him.

"Is it Jim?"

A jab of realization spiked his gut. He couldn't keep anything from Mama. She knew him too well. Jim, his faithful worker and friend, had hinted several times about his daughter and grandsons. "Maybe."

"Take that to the Lord, son."

Gideon looked up at the heavens. "I'm trying, Mama. But Jim's right. Maria does need some help."

"God provides in His ways. We don't need to fix things that aren't ours to fix." Mama patted his arm before she walked into the house.

Gideon stared at the clouds that lay serenely in the sky. Maria was a wonderful Christian woman, and Gideon adored her two sons. Widowed, she took care of the boys and worked hard at her job. But she struggled, and it was hard for Jim to watch.

Jim had worked the orchard for years—the last two with Gideon, and two decades before that with Gideon's mentor. Jim had his own ideas of how to help Maria. They involved Gideon and a lifetime commitment. Jim liked the idea. Maria seemed okay with it. The boys would probably be fine with it.

But Gideon just wasn't so sure.

two

Lydia couldn't remember the last time she'd been so embarrassed. Well, in truth, it hadn't been *that* long ago. The first remembrance that came to mind was when she went to the hospital to help her friend who'd just had a baby load up her things to go home. Lydia had found a bowl of sorts and filled it with several toiletries. When an unbelievably handsome male nurse came in and chuckled, Lydia couldn't figure out what was wrong.

"It's a bedpan." The nurse laughed, pointing at the container. Lydia dumped out the contents as the guy continued to chuckle. "At least it was new."

Lydia shook the memory from her mind. At least she hadn't told the nurse that she and his mother had been talking about how cute he was! Warmth spread up her cheeks, and she quickened her pace as she remembered how Gideon's expression had changed from anger to embarrassment to humor as she fumbled over her words.

She scaled the steps to the front door and walked inside. She sat George down on the floor and stared down at him. "Are you going to cause this kind of trouble every day?" He winked, a reflex surely, and wagged his tail. "Great. Even my puppy thinks I'm funny."

After flopping on the couch, Lydia slipped off her shoes. She turned and lay back, resting her head on the arm cushion. Gideon looked like an adorable, scruffy farmer. His worn jeans had dirt patches at his hips where he'd obviously wiped his hands. His somewhat-white T-shirt couldn't hide his broad shoulders. His sandy brown hair and facial stubble were actually a shade lighter than the kiss the sun had given his face and arms. The mixture caused his eyes, a swirling of green, hazel, and brown, to pop. A chill raced through her. *He has amazing eyes.*

"Knock it off." She smacked her hands against the cushion beside her hips. George barked and jumped on the couch beside her. He tried to lick her hand, but she swatted him away. "No more kisses. I'm mad at you, remember?"

He ignored her words and nestled his nose beneath her hand. She couldn't help but giggle when his wet nose reached her palm. "All right, little guy." She picked him up and wiggled him back and forth. "Down you go." She set him on the floor then leaned back again.

She had no business thinking of Lorma's son in such a way. He may have looked scruffy, but he was obviously meticulous when it came to his fruits. Lydia Hammond and meticulous did not get along well, as Lydia's perfect mother would have no problem pointing out. Lydia always messed things up, and thinking about Gideon's eyes was a mess-up waiting to happen.

She started to count the pointy parts in the spackle on the ceiling. By the time she got to ten she laughed out loud at the ridiculous activity. *Hmm.* She rested her hands behind her head. This spot would be much more comfortable than the floor to do crunches. *I'm sure it's not as effective, but if I do an extra ten or twenty, maybe I'll get the same results without killing my back.*

She maneuvered herself until her head and her feet lay

flat on the couch. Placing her palms behind her head, she intertwined her fingers. *Definitely not a firm foundation, but hopefully it will still be effective.*

Slowly, she lifted her head and chest. "One." She lay back and inhaled. Up and exhale. "Two." Back and inhale. Up and exhale. "Three." She continued several more times. "This hurts my back worse." She flopped against the couch.

"That's because you're supposed to do it on a hard surface."

Lydia jumped up and screamed. A man had broken into the house! She grabbed the first thing in her reach and threw it at him. The tall figure ducked as a sofa pillow flew past his head.

Lydia gasped when she recognized Lorma's son. "What are you doing here?" She frowned as she noted he held her dog's leash in one hand and her puppy in the other. "And how did you get in?"

"Well, I came to return this." He handed George's leash to her. "And your pup was digging in your flowers, so I picked him up, as well." He raised his eyebrows and cocked his head. "Am I to assume this little guy got out of the house without you knowing it?"

Lydia blew a wisp of hair from her eyes. "Yes. I don't know how he managed to get the door open." She sighed. "I must not have closed it all the way."

"I know a really good obedience trainer."

Hurt welled inside of Lydia. Her dog messed up his peaches. She can't close a door. She's the only goof who does crunches on a couch. Now she can't train a pup. Flighty, her mother called her. Irresponsible. Lydia liked to think of descriptions like spontaneous and adventurous. On the other hand, when her mother asked her when she would ever be content to settle down, Lydia started evaluating her life. Contentment was what she wanted, more than anything. She wanted to find something and be happy. Jesus had given her a contentment she'd never known, and yet she still grew restless as she searched for God's purpose for her life.

"You don't have to take him to a trainer. You could train him yourself." Gideon put George on the floor.

"I doubt it," Lydia muttered.

"Sure you could. There're lots of dog obedience books on the Internet and at the library."

Lydia studied Gideon's face. He had a scar, probably an inch long, above his right eye at his hairline. Its whiteness stood in contrast to his sun-darkened skin. But it was his eyes and the sincerity shining from them that held her captive. They didn't seem to swirl together as they had before. The green framed his pupil while the hazel wrapped around the green and the deep brown circled the hazel. Like a bull's-eye. "Do your eyes change with your mood?"

Gideon's eyebrows met in a line as a smile curled his lips.

Lydia bit her bottom lip and scrunched her nose. She'd said that out loud. Yep, she'd asked him *out loud* if his eyes change. Foolish mouth. Foolish, nonstop-getting-me-into-trouble mouth. How many scriptures were there that focused on that nemesis—the tongue—and how many times had she read them? And yet, she still said whatever happened to be on her mind the moment she thought it!

"Yeah. People do tell me my eyes change. Mama can look at my eyes and instantly know what kind of mood I'm in, almost what I'm thinking even."

Lydia giggled and blinked slowly. "What does a bull's-eye mean?" *Oh my. I just flirted with him. I just blatantly flirted with him. Please, God, help me here. I'm digging myself deeper and deeper.*

The phone rang, and Lydia jumped. "Oh. I better get the phone. Thanks for bringing the leash back."

She started to turn away, but Gideon touched her arm. She peered up at him. The green around his pupils deepened. "It means I've seen something that put a smile on my face, something I like." He winked, then turned and walked out the door.

Lydia watched him. What had he seen today—her dog mutilate his peaches and her flowers? He'd witnessed her fumble every word she spoke. Oh, yes, and he had seen her doing crunches on the living room sofa. She'd given him plenty to smile about all right. He'd probably be laughing the whole way home. And yet his eyes didn't quite express teasing. It was something...

The phone rang again. Lydia shook her head and ran into the kitchen toward the phone. She picked it up. "Hello."

"Hi, Lydia. It's Mom."

"Mom!" Lydia smiled and swallowed at the same time. She loved her mother. With all her heart she loved her, but her mom rarely saw the good in Lydia. At least that's how Lydia felt. Her mom was a successful lawyer in Indianapolis with plans to run for state office the next term. And what was Lydia? Right now, unemployed and trying to learn more about the God she'd given her life to and what He wanted for her.

"I just got back from visiting Allison and the girls."

Lydia cringed. Her older sister had two beautiful school-age daughters and her own dental practice in a small town in Kentucky. "How are they doing?"

"They're terrific. You should think about visiting them.

Maybe Allison can give you some ideas."

Lydia chose not to ask what kinds of ideas. She already knew her mother meant business ideas. Something that would make Lydia stable and successful. The problem remained that Lydia just wasn't sure what God wanted. "I've enjoyed Grandma's house. I painted the downstairs bath—"

"Oh, good. That's what I wanted to talk with you about. I'm planning to stop by for a visit on Friday."

"Friday?"

"I can only stay until Sunday afternoon, but I wanted to see you about Grandma's house. You know how your Aunt Grace is. She wanted me to make sure you weren't changing anything in Grandma's house."

"I haven't, Mom. The house belongs to you and Aunt Grace. I know that, and I would never do anything to hurt Gran—"

"I know, but I need to make sure. My beeper is going off. I'll see you Friday."

The phone went dead. Lydia pulled it away from her ear and stared at the numbers. No "How are you doing?" No "I love you." Just "I need to make sure you're not hurting Grandma's house." Lydia sighed. She longed for a better relationship with her mother.

And her Aunt Grace. Lydia huffed. So much for a name fitting a person. Her aunt had anything but grace. Well, that wasn't exactly true. Her aunt was an exquisite entertainer. She knew all the "right" people and all the "right" things to say and do in front of them, but she remained clueless when it came to exhibiting grace. Her aunt had never been one to put up with the recklessness or misbehavior of others. Including Lydia.

God, how did I get into this family? I know if I settled into a job, Mom would be happy. Aunt Grace, too, I suppose. I understand Mom's frustrations with me. I've been a little bit of everything over the years. Even now, I'm living on money Grandma left me in her will. Really, it's not very practical. I've changed since I met You, but I'm still not. . .

Lydia sighed and hung up the phone. She walked to the kitchen, opened the refrigerator, and grabbed a bottle of water. After taking a quick drink, she shut the door and peered at one of her grandmother's magnets. Grandma didn't really fit into the family either. In fact, Lydia was a lot like her grandmother. She read the verse on the magnet quietly at first. Allowing the meaning to sink in, she read it again, aloud. "'For I know the plans I have for you,' declares the Lord, 'plans to prosper you and not to harm you, plans to give you hope and a future.'"

God, You have a plan for me. One that is especially designed for me. I trust You to show me in Your time.

ॐ

Gideon chuckled as he made his way back to his house. He hadn't intended to scare Lydia when he went into her home. His hands were full with a pup and a leash, and since the door was open and he couldn't knock, he thought he'd just step inside. He hadn't expected to see her doing crunches on her couch. Crunches, for crying out loud. He laughed again.

That woman was interesting. He'd have to give her that. He couldn't deny she was quite attractive, as well. Usually freckles were not one of his favorite physical traits, but something about hers enhanced her appearance. Maybe it wasn't the freckles. Maybe it was the ice blue eyes or that cute, slightly upturned nose.

But she was flighty, too. He scratched the stubble on his chin. No, not really flighty, but spontaneous. Yes, he liked that description much better. He'd met her only an hour ago, and already he had no idea what to expect her to say or do. He liked that. She lightened his mood and brightened his afternoon. If only her phone hadn't rung, he would have loved to spend a bit more time getting to know her. *Or getting to know what she thinks about the way I look.* Gideon laughed again. She couldn't keep her honesty to herself if she tried. He liked that, too. She was genuine. Already he could tell she was the real deal.

"Hey, Gideon, where'd you run off to?" Jim's scratchy voice sounded from up ahead. "Something funny happen?"

Gideon cleared his throat. "No. I just had to run something back to our neighbor for Mama."

"I see." Jim looked back at Lydia's house. "Marian's grand-daughter's awful pretty, wouldn't you say?"

Gideon shrugged. He had no reason to feel uneasy. Jim was his employee, but lately Jim had been too consumed with Gideon and Maria and matrimony. "She's attractive, I suppose."

Jim shoved his hands in his pockets. " 'Course, she has plenty of means to provide for herself. Her mom, her grandma, God rest her soul. . . . She even has a good home to live in."

Gideon closed his eyes. *Here we go.*

"My Maria has to rent a tiny one-bedroom apartment for her and the boys. She does all she can, but. . ."

"I'll be happy to help her out with groceries or clothes."

Jim balked. "She won't take no charity. She's a good Christian woman who'd work hard alongside a good Christian man."

Gideon stopped and turned toward his employee. "What

are you trying to say, Jim? Why don't you just—"

Jim turned away and swiped a leaf off a tree. "I'm just saying the Bible tells us to care for widows and such. My Maria is a widow—a kind, caring, attractive lady."

"I agree, and I would love to help her out. But if you're talking about commit—"

Jim laughed and swatted the air. "I'm not talking about anything particularly. Just mentioning the facts." He rubbed his hands together. "Having to move those boys away from their home in Wisconsin after their daddy's death has been hard on all of them. But they've had time enough to grieve."

"Jim, it's only been eight months. I've spent my life letting God lead my love life, and I don't feel comfortable rushing into—"

"Oh, come on now." Jim patted Gideon's shoulder. "Let's not think of that. How'd we get on that to begin with? A man couldn't work for anyone better." Jim let go of Gideon's shoulder and walked on ahead.

Gideon watched him for several seconds. *God, what do I do about this? Do You want me to think of Maria in the way Jim wants? Show me.*

He moved ahead. Within moments, the bushes rustled beside him. Gideon looked over, expecting to find a squirrel. Instead, Kelbe, Maria's five-year-old son, jumped out and wrapped his arms around Gideon's waist. Giggling, Jeremy, the three-year-old, scurried around the bush and wrapped himself around Gideon's leg. Gideon laughed as he tried to move forward. "Oh no, I've been attacked, but I am stronger than these little creatures."

Kelbe slid down to wrap himself around Gideon's free leg. Gideon walked like Frankenstein's monster toward the house.

.

"You may think you can beat me," Gideon wailed, "but I am stronger than the both of you together."

"Let's get him, Jer," Kelbe hollered as he rose up and started to tickle Gideon's waist.

"You can't win, I say." Gideon bent down and tickled Kelbe's stomach. Jeremy tried to jump on Gideon's back, but Gideon turned and tickled him, as well.

The game went on for several minutes until Jeremy and Kelbe fell over from exhaustion. Gideon took several deep breaths, as well. No amount of work or exercise could top a five-minute tickle match with Maria's boys. "How 'bout you two run up to the house and ask Mrs. Andrews for a drink of lemonade?"

"Yeah!" Jeremy rolled his chubby legs to a standing position then raced for the house. "Miz Adrew. Wemoade!"

"What?" His mother's voice filled the air. He could see her confused expression even from a distance.

Kelbe hopped up and ran for the porch. "Gideon said we could have some lemonade."

Gideon watched his mom smile. "Well, sure. Get in here." She opened the back door and disappeared inside with the boys.

After one long breath, Gideon wiped most of the dirt from his shirt and jeans. "They're a handful, huh?"

Gideon turned toward the voice. He smiled at Maria. "Yes, they are, but in a good way."

"Hmm. Try getting them in bed at night. It's an hour-long process." She grinned, exposing deep dimples on both sides of her cheeks.

Gideon took in her shoulder-length dark hair. By all accounts, it appeared very soft. She had a lovely smile, straight white teeth. Her eyes were a bit of a dull green; however, their shape was quite attractive.

But there was no spark—no gut desire to get to know her better.

She was a wonderful person. A great friend. Had adorable kids. But that was all. He didn't feel anything else. Didn't know if he could ever feel anything else.

Gideon scratched his stubble. "I'm sure you're a very patient person."

Maria gazed at the ground. Gideon noted that her eyelashes were so long they seemed to touch her cheek with the motion. *That's a really attractive thing—long eyelashes. Most of my buddies love it when ladies bat their lashes.* And yet, Gideon felt nothing.

"Your mom invited us for dinner." She traced a line in the dirt with her sandal. "For all I know, Daddy invited us." She looked up, and Gideon couldn't decipher the meaning of her words. Did she feel frustrated with her dad or did she agree with him? "Anyway, I hope you don't mind."

Gideon clapped his hands then rubbed them together. "Of course I don't mind. You and the boys are always welcome, but I'm starving. I hope dinner's ready."

"It is." Maria grinned. "It's your favorite." She winked. "I helped."

Gideon's stomach plummeted. She was the second woman to flirt with him today. This time, however, he didn't feel hungry for more. Instead, he'd lost his appetite.

three

Before George's barks had time to reach their full tirade, Lydia heard gravel popping in the driveway, no doubt signaling the arrival of a new, sleek Mercedes. After scooping the pup into her hand, Lydia peeked past the ivory lace curtain.

A force, often stronger than the winds of a thunderstorm, stepped out of the polished silver vehicle. Rita Louise Hammond wore a fitted navy suit, white button-down blouse with an oversized collar, and shiny red heels. A red strap that connected perfectly into a small navy purse rested obediently on her shoulder.

Lydia could hear her mother's confident voice in the back of her mind. "A bit of red to a woman's attire does the same as a red tie for a man." She'd raise one eyebrow and smirk. "Expresses power."

Lydia glanced down at her gray, cutoff sweatpants and Indiana University T-shirt. Why hadn't she dressed in a nice pair of capris and a summer sweater, or a pair of decent shorts at least? She knew her mom would come dressed to the nines. *It's no wonder she thinks I'm irresponsible. I'd think I'd have more sense than to dress like this knowing she was coming.*

She blew a stray curl from the front of her face. *Oh, well. This is who I am.* She peeked back through the window and watched as her mother studied the chewed-on daylily. Lydia had tried to conjure life and uprightness from the poor foliage George had demolished, but remnants of the pup's presence remained. Her mom frowned and rubbed her lips with her index finger. A proven sign of her aggravation.

Deciding she might as well get their greeting over with, Lydia opened the front door and walked outside. "Hi, Mom. I'm glad you came."

Her mom screamed and swatted at her right thigh. She jumped from one foot to the other, smacking her leg, her chest, then her face. Lydia felt her mouth drop open as she stood in shocked silence while her mother blew air from her lips and blinked several times. Finally, still running in place, she shook her head, messing her hair with her fingertips.

"Mom. . ."

"What was that?" Her mom's eyes glazed with fear. She rested her palm against her chest. Her gaze sought the ground around her. "There it is."

Lydia watched as her mother stomped on a beetle and ground it into the earth. She'd never seen the woman so erratic and upset. She knew her mouth still gaped open, but she couldn't seem to shut it.

"There." Her mother breathed out and swiped her hand through her hair then pressed her crisp pants. She looked up. Surprise filled her mother's eyes when Lydia made eye contact with her. One side of her mom's mouth lifted slightly.

Lydia couldn't stop the gurgling that formed in her stomach and made its way up her chest and into her throat. It started as a slight giggle, but when her mother's soft laugh filled the air, Lydia lost her composure and burst into deep, gut-wrenching laughter.

It took several moments, but Lydia got herself together and gave her mom a hug. "I am glad to see you."

"I see you have a friend." Rita petted George's head.

Lydia marveled at her mom's tenderness. Reveling the moment, she pointed toward the disheveled flowers. "Yes, George is the little scamp who decided to chew on my garden."

Her mom's mood darkened, and she headed toward the door. "Well, I hope he hasn't damaged any of Mother's furniture."

"Oh, he hasn't." Lydia followed behind. Why had she brought her mother's attention back toward those flowers? She shook her head.

"You said you painted Mother's bathroom?"

Lydia hadn't realized her mother had paid any attention to her saying it over the phone. "Yes. I painted it a—"

"Upstairs or downstairs?"

"Downstairs." Lydia released a slow sigh as Rita's heels clicked against hardwood toward the bathroom. Her mother was back to her usual self. Critical. Formal. Nothing at all like Lydia. *God, will we ever be able to see eye-to-eye, or agree on anything for that matter?*

"Purple!"

Her mother's exclamation echoed through the house. Lydia rolled her eyes. "It's not purple, Mom."

Rita stuck her head out the door. She lifted her eyebrows and pierced Lydia with a scowl. "Surely you know your colors, Lydia Anne."

"I know my colors!" Anger welled within her, and it took all her strength not to stomp toward the small room. "It's a light plum, and if you look beside the vanity, you'll notice I hung one of Grandma's favorite pictures. I matched the walls with the color of the girl's dress."

Mom snarled. "I don't know why Mother always liked this cheap, old picture, but I suppose it looks all right in here." She walked out of the bathroom.

Lydia held tight to George as she followed her mother around the house. Rita had a comment for every speck of dust, every rumpled pillow, every scratch on the floors, and on and on.

Lydia felt she would scream before her mother finally made it into the kitchen. Trying to add something positive to the visit, Lydia pointed toward the counter. "I made a pie for you."

"Yes. I thought I smelled something."

Lydia knew the mixture of apples and cinnamon was tantalizing, but, as usual, her mother couldn't seem to bring herself to say anything nice. "I'll just put George in the backyard. . ."

"Honestly, Lydia, I don't know why you didn't do that to begin with."

Lydia put the pup in the backyard before heading to the sink to wash her hands. "Have a seat, Mom." She nodded toward the table she'd arranged in front of the oversized bay window.

The view of some of Indiana's best land spilled through those panes. She loved living in Danville. Lydia could gaze at Grandma's flower gardens and farther past them to the grass, trees, and wildflowers that seemed to go on forever.

"Make sure you use plenty of soap. I don't want that creature's germs on the food."

"Of course." Lydia had to bite her lip to keep from saying anything disrespectful. God instructed her to honor her mother, but sometimes it was just plain hard.

She took a knife from the drawer and sliced through the pie. Perfect, it was still just a tad warm when she laid the pieces on the plates she'd already set out. After grabbing the ice cream from the refrigerator, she dropped a scoop to the right of each slice. Lydia took the desserts and utensils and sat across from her mom. She forced a slight smile at her mom then focused on her pie. *Mmm, this is good.* She had added just a touch more sugar this time, and Lydia felt surprised at what a difference such a small amount made.

"Lydia Anne. . ."

Lydia exhaled. What could her mother possibly want to berate her about now?

"This is the best pie I've ever tasted."

"What?"

"Lydia, this is wonderful. I knew you were good, but this. . . it's better than Mother's."

"Better than Grandma's? Oh no, no. . ."

"Yes, it is." Her mother leaned over and grabbed Lydia's hand. "You should consider selling these. You'd make a fortune." She fell back against her chair and laughed. "I've been so worried about you wasting your life. One job after another, and here you have a domestic talent. I mean I knew you liked to bake, but who'd have thought a daughter of mine could do it this well?" She snorted. "Hammond women are meant to be powerhouses, pillars of their community, and here I've raised a Betty Crocker."

Lydia was afraid to let her mind believe what her heart felt. Sure, her mother almost meant the compliment as an insult. Not a new concept in Lydia's life, but still her mother thought she had talent, that she was good at something. For the first time in her memory, Lydia had pleased her mother. Lydia relished the moment. She liked it. She liked it a lot.

❧

Gideon tucked the dog obedience books he'd purchased under

his arm. He'd intentionally picked the cheapest ones he could find on the Internet, not because of the price but because they were the most used. He didn't want Lydia to think she'd filled his thoughts the last few days and that he was desperate to do anything to see her again. If she happened to believe he'd had the books around the house for a while, that would work for him. Of course, if she came right out and asked, he'd never lie. *It's not really even a lie of omission, because why would she care where I got the books?*

No, it's more about motive.

He shook his head against the unwanted thought. He'd just give her the books, not overanalyze why, how, when, or what he got them for. He'd just give them to her. Just see her again. Just hear her fumble over her words. He grinned.

Her house came into sight. The mile walk proved not only good exercise, but since he didn't need to take his truck anywhere, he didn't have to tell anyone where he was going. They assumed he was hard at work in the orchard. No one, Jim especially, would ask him any questions. Man, how he'd become tired of questions and suggestions.

A ball of fur bounced through the grass a ways in front of him. "What in the world?" Soon he heard the half yelp, half bark of Lydia's puppy. "Hello there, George." Gideon bent down and picked the little guy up. As before, the pup tried to lick his hand, his arm, any surface of body the pup could find. "You're friendly, I'll give you that."

Gideon walked the rest of the distance to her house. Now he had two reasons to see her. He headed to her porch, but before he could knock, the door opened and Lydia stepped outside. "Hi, Gideon."

An unexpected thrill raced through him at the sound of his

name from her lips. He blinked. *I've lost my mind. Some weird sickness has overtaken my thoughts and made me a sap.*

Lydia put her hands on her hips. "George, I've been looking everywhere for you."

Even her reprimand to the little fur ball proved the cutest thing he'd seen in a while. Gideon didn't know what it was about Lydia, but he couldn't quite reach his fill of seeing her. The pup barked. Gideon forced himself back to reality and handed the pup to Lydia. "He must have gotten out again."

Brilliant line, Andrews. Way to impress the girl.

Lydia shook her head. Gideon couldn't help but notice the sun dance across the red and blond strands of her hair. *Wow! What a gorgeous color!* Her cheeks blazed pink, setting off the blue in her eyes. Either she felt embarrassed the dog had gotten out again or she was furious with the little critter. No matter what, he needed to get his head straight and form sentences that were at the very least conversational.

Her face fell into the most adorable pout he'd ever witnessed. The woman would be able to get him to purchase the moon simply with the expressions of her face. "There's got to be a hole in the fence in the backyard. I don't know how he's doing it."

A job, yes. If he had a purpose, a reason to help her, then maybe his mind wouldn't race off so much. "I don't mind taking a look for you."

"No, no. You've helped enough. Thanks for bringing George back." Her eyes widened and her skin turned white. "Don't tell me he'd run all the way to your house."

Gideon shook his head. "No." He looked down at the books. "I was heading over here to bring you some books on obedience."

She frowned.

He cleared his throat. "Remember we'd talked about. . ."

Her eyebrows lifted and her lips bowed into the prettiest shape he'd ever seen. "That's right. Thank you." She took them from his hand. "Did you get these on the Internet for me?"

Gideon puckered his lips. *Now who asks that? Who even thinks to ask if something was purchased on the Internet? They're used. Most people would believe them to be the giver's property.* Gideon sighed. Not Lydia. She was too open, too honest with her thoughts. He'd have a hard time tricking her with anything. Her innocence would pick up on it.

I'll tell her if she asks. It's not a lie of omission. His own thoughts smacked him in the face. *Okay, God. I was trying to be sneaky. She called me out on it. Forgive me, Lord.*

"Yes, I did buy them for you."

"Why?"

"To apologize for the way I'd behaved." *Sorry again, God. Not exactly true, but now that I think about it, I'm glad I bought them as a means to say I'm sorry.*

"Oh." The questioning look on her face just about had him unglued. He had to think of a way to change the subject. He noticed the Mercedes. "Very nice car. Didn't know you had a Mercedes."

She blew a strand of hair from her eyes. A beautiful gesture, like blades of wheat blowing with the wind, only much prettier. Gideon lost the beginning of her response. Somewhere he thought he heard her say "mother." He asked, "So, it's your mom's car?"

She frowned again. "That's what I said." She placed her hand back on her hip. "Are you all right?"

"I'm fine." Gideon noticed she had five freckles on her nose.

Well, several little ones, as well, but five that he could really count. Three kind of clumped together on one side while the other two spread out a bit on the other side. Very cute.

"I asked if you wanted a piece of pie."

Gideon scratched the stubble at his jaw. He had to stop staring at the woman. He'd scare her to death if he didn't act more like a gentleman. "I'd love a piece of your pie."

He followed her through the living room and into the kitchen. She turned around and almost ran into him. Almost, but not quite. He would have loved a reason to wrap his arms around her for a second.

She motioned toward the table. "My mom's asleep in the spare bedroom upstairs. She's spending the weekend with me."

"That's nice." By the pained expression that wrapped her face, Gideon wondered if it wasn't such a nice thing.

Lydia laid the plate of pie on the table. It smelled good, and he wondered where she'd bought it. He took a bite. "This is terrific." He jammed his fork back into the piece and shoveled pie into his mouth. "Where did you get this?"

"I told you I made it."

"When?"

"Out on the porch."

When I started daydreaming about freckles, no doubt. "Well, this is really good."

A slight blush tinted her cheeks, and her eyes smiled contentedly with her lips. "You're the second person to say that today. Thank you."

In all his twenty-eight years, Gideon had never felt such an urge to kiss a woman. He didn't know it was possible for a man to go "cuckoo," as he and his brothers used to tease their sisters. Somehow, this lady who couldn't keep track of her dog, whom he'd only met one time before, this woman, who'd captured his mother's heart, had also captured his.

He loved the idea of it.

❧

It was almost eleven when Lydia crawled into her bed. She couldn't seem to shake the pleasure that filled her heart with her mother's and Gideon's approvals over her pie. Her mother's commendation remained especially sweet.

She picked up her Bible. Before Sam left, Lydia had promised her friend that she'd read through the New Testament. Lydia had made it all the way to First Thessalonians. She wondered at all she'd learned about God. Some things still confused her. Sam had told her that would be true until they reached heaven. Even with questions, God had strengthened her faith in Him. Already, she couldn't imagine living life, even living a day, without Him.

After grabbing her pen and pad on the nightstand, Lydia opened her Bible. She began reading about the book of Thessalonians, that it had been Paul's letter to the city of Thessalonica. She started reading the verses, making notes on her pad. She read through chapter one and on to chapter two. She stopped at verse four and frowned. She read it again. *What are You telling me here, Lord?*

She read the verse one more time aloud. " 'On the contrary, we speak as men approved by God to be entrusted with the gospel. We are not trying to please men but God, who tests our hearts.' " She shut the book and closed her eyes.

Not trying to please men. Not trying to please men. A lone tear spilled down her cheek. She swiped at it, causing more to fall. "Oh God, I've been so consumed with pleasing men. Well, Mom, more than anyone, but I'm consumed with it. I always have been. I've felt like a failure in her eyes."

Lydia reached for a tissue on the nightstand. She wiped her nose and her eyes. "I am to please You. Oh Jesus, forgive me. Mom doesn't know You. I need to be a witness to her. I thought pleasing her would make me a good witness, but that's wrong." She had to stop to blow her nose. "Pleasing You is what will make me a good witness. Forgive me, Lord. Help me to seek Your pleasure above everything. I love You, Lord."

Lydia jotted the scripture down in her notepad. She flipped through the pages before noting all the verses she wanted to commit to memory. Her gaze found one from Galatians that mimicked the Thessalonians verse. Without a doubt, God wanted her to please Him, and Him alone. She closed her Bible and turned off the light. She wanted to chew on the verse while she slept. She wanted to evaluate where her talents were, where her pleasures were. She wanted to sit still and listen to what God had to say.

She no longer wanted to live to please men.

She wanted to please God.

four

"Am I now trying to win the approval of men, or of God? Or am I trying to please men? If I were still trying to please men, I would not be a servant of Christ."

Gideon stopped and listened to the animated voice playing from his mother's Bible CD. The narrator continued on. Gideon could tell by the flavor of the words that the writer was Paul, but he didn't know which book was being read. He searched through the kitchen and into the living area until he finally found his mother cleaning pictures in the hall. "What book of the Bible are you listening to, Mama?"

"Look at this picture." She held up one that displayed his entire family before Pa died. "Remember this?"

"Yes. It was Kylie's wedding. But which book of the Bible are you listening to?"

His mama shook her head, swatting her hand in front of her face. He knew she lamented his father, probably missed her other children, as well. "I can't remember. I'll go look."

She shoved the picture in his hand and walked back into the kitchen. A twinge of sadness, maybe even loneliness, tugged at his heart. His pa's death had been hard, but at the same time, Pa had been so miserably sick. It felt almost crueler to pray for Pa to have more time on this earth. Pa rejoiced with angels and saints in heaven now. Of that, Gideon remained sure.

And yet, as time passed, over two years now, Gideon found himself missing Pa more, not less. It seemed odd to him.

Wrong, in some way. Maybe it was because seeing Pa so sick proved harder than seeing him die. Maybe as time drifted by, Gideon remembered the times Pa had been healthy more often than the times he had been ill.

Gideon looked at the picture in his hand. With his thumb, he caressed the brass frame. Pa had been sick in this picture, yet he was smiling. He felt so happy, so proud that Kylie had found a wonderful Christian man. The whole family loved Ryan. Ryan had been Gideon's greatest encourager while he went to college to major in agriculture. Not only had he encouraged, he'd financially aided, as well.

Gideon looked back at the expressions on his parents' faces. Mama's smile was apparent, even though her face was turned as she looked at her husband of so many years. Pure pleasure wrapped her expression. His pa smiled at the camera, content and happy as could be. No one who looked at this picture would have known black lung already tore away at his insides, leaving him sick and unstable, especially at night.

But that wasn't how Gideon remembered Pa. He didn't think of him in terms of this picture or the all-too-short years that followed. He thought of him on the front porch of their old house, strong and healthy, playing the guitar and singing hymns as loud as his deep voice could muster. Gideon remembered him playing basketball with them when they were teenagers and playing the card game of war with them when they were young.

A memory of Pa standing behind Mama as she washed the dishes flooded his mind. Pa had leaned down and kissed Mama's cheek, and the lot of them, probably five of the eight kids, saw the show of affection and squealed in protest. Pa only chuckled while Mama shooed him away.

He wanted a love like that.

"It's Galatians," Mama's voice sounded from down the hall. "I'm listening to Galatians."

Gideon blinked back to reality and hung the picture back on its nail. "Thanks, Mama." He headed toward the stairs. He had a few minutes before he needed to get back to the orchard. A quick peek at Galatians wouldn't take much time.

"Lorma! Gideon! Someone!" A scream sounded from the yard. Gideon raced out the front door to find Maria sitting on the ground, holding three-year-old Jeremy in her arms. Blood patched his shirt and pants as well as the front of her shirt. Crying, Kelbe stood beside them holding a three-foot pipe with blood covering one end.

"What happened?" Gideon scooped the boy out of her arms and raced to the bathroom. "Where is he bleeding?"

Maria ran behind him. "His thumb."

"It was a accident," Kelbe mumbled through tears. Maria must have been holding him now, as well.

"What's wrong?" Mama yelled.

"Get some towels, Mama." Gideon placed the child's bloody hand under the faucet. Turning on the cold, he hoped it was just a small wound, maybe needing a few stitches. A large chunk of Jeremy's thumb flapped over, and Gideon thought he would vomit. Pushing the flesh back, Gideon grabbed one of the towels Mama had gotten and wrapped it around Jeremy's thumb. "Start the truck. We're going to the emergency room."

"No, my car has his car seat. I just don't think I can—" Maria looked down at her shirt and tears welled in her eyes. "I don't think I can drive."

"Give me your keys." Gideon held the towel around Jeremy's thumb while Maria searched her purse. The blood seemed to have stopped quickly. Gideon hoped that was a good thing.

Once he had the keys, only a matter of moments passed until the two boys, Maria, and Gideon were buckled into seats and Gideon was driving to the nearest hospital.

"How did this happen?" Gideon asked Kelbe. The vision of the five-year-old holding the pipe sent cold chills up his spine. If Gideon's guess proved right, it was the device his mother purchased, which was meant to go under the doorknob to help keep perpetrators out. But it was missing the rubber parts that went on each end. When Pa died, Mama had bought one for each of the doors. What was Kelbe doing with it?

"We were playing with Mrs. Andrews's door thingy."

Yep, just as Gideon suspected.

Kelbe went on. "I pulled the bendy parts off, and we were jumping over it, trying to see who could jump the highest." Kelbe's voice cracked, and Gideon looked in the rearview mirror to see his lower lip shake. "I didn't mean for Jer to get hurt. I didn't. . ."

"It was an accident." Maria's voice remained calm and reassuring as she patted her oldest son's leg with her free hand. She held the towel around Jeremy's thumb with the other.

"Yes, Kelbe. It was an accident." Gideon added, "I should've had Mama get rid of those things when she moved here. The rubber pieces are constantly coming off."

Maria looked at Gideon. Her eyes shone with her appreciation for supporting her son. The expression felt intimate, more so than Gideon really felt comfortable with. He cared about the boys, and Maria for that matter. Of course he wouldn't say anything to hurt them, but he wasn't sure he wanted expressions like that.

They made it to the hospital, and Gideon carried Jeremy into the emergency room. Maria and Kelbe followed behind. Once inside, Gideon handed Jeremy to Maria and allowed her to take care of all the registration forms. He grabbed Kelbe's hand and led him to a vending machine. After the little guy purchased a snack and drink, they sat together in front of the lobby television.

"I'm glad you helped us." Kelbe kicked his legs, which couldn't quite reach the floor, beneath the chair. "Mommy was real scared."

"I think she was doing all right." Gideon tried to re-assure him.

"No. Mommy don't like blood. Makes her sick."

"Your mom's a tough lady."

"No." Kelbe shook his head. "One time I got bit by a dog when I was four." Kelbe lifted his face and pointed to a scar beneath his eye. "Mommy fell down and fell asleep. Daddy had to take me to see the doctor." Kelbe lowered his face and dug his hand back into his bag of pretzels. "Daddy's not here no more though."

Gideon's heart broke for the little guy, for both little guys. They needed a dad. Gideon knew how important a good father was in a boy's life. He'd had one of the best ever.

Lord, are You trying to tell me something?

❧

Lydia looked at her watch. "Ugh. It's almost eleven and I still haven't made it to the grocery." Her stomach gurgled from a lack of breakfast, and her head had a small drummer inside it, beating ever so softly yet consistently against her brain.

She hadn't had her morning coffee and bowl of oatmeal, and she could feel Mr. Grouch shaking his fist up at her from the trash can inside her gut.

She'd spent the week since Mother left going through Grandma's attic. As a pleasant surprise, she'd found the sweetest painting of a small boy sitting on a garden stool holding a bug of some kind. A faithful pup sat beside him. The lavender flowers in the background of the painting matched the bathroom she'd painted perfectly, so she'd taken the treasure to a framer to select a mat and frame.

That had been two hours ago!

She pulled into a parking space at the grocery and turned off the engine. "Who'd have thought it would take so long to pick out a picture frame," she growled as she pulled her ponytail holder out of her hair, ran her fingers through her wayward curls, and fixed the ponytail again. Believing she'd be in and out of town in one hour at the most, she hadn't fixed her makeup or put on decent clothing. She was covered in a wrinkled T-shirt, neon pink slippers adorning her feet, and her long, flannel pajama pants—multicolored polka dots over stripes. What had beguiled her to buy such an atrocious pair of pants? She nodded her head, remembering. They were a gag gift from a college friend. She lifted one eyebrow. . .she'd bought the neon shoes herself.

Oh well, what does it matter what a gal looks like? Isn't beauty about what's inside? She giggled. Most people would at least allow others to see the beauty of being dressed in daytime clothes when coming to town. She held back a snort. The clothes were the least of her worries. She'd die if any-one spoke to her; she hadn't even brushed her teeth. She thought she could drop the picture off and that was that, but no, she had to select various shades, sizes, and whatnot. It's a wonder the framer didn't keel over from her foulness.

"Mother would be appalled." She spoke to her reflection in the visor mirror. After rubbing the front of her teeth with her finger, she pinched her cheeks for some color. "We're not trying to impress men," she announced with confident flair. Looking to the heavens, she added, "But I guess that doesn't count when it comes to brushing my teeth. I could have at least done that."

She *would* just head right back to her house, shower, and come back, but she didn't have any coffee at home, and the little drummer guy would not leave her poor brain alone until she did something to feed him.

With a shrug of her shoulders, Lydia flung her purse on her arm and hopped out of her car. The chances of seeing anyone she would know were slim to none. She'd only been to church twice. Outside of the Andrews, she really hadn't met anyone. *Really, it's highly unlikely I'll see. . .*

"Lydia, is that you?" A sweet voice sounded from behind her.

No way. It is not possible. Lydia turned ever so slowly. *Please let her be alone. Please let her be alone.* It wasn't like Lydia had spent *all* her waking hours thinking of Gideon Andrews and his sandy hair and scruffy face that made him appear so manly. No, she'd spent a whole lot of her sleeping hours thinking about him, as well. "Hello, Mrs. Andrews." She spied her friend. Alone. *Thank You, Jesus.*

"I told you to call me Lorma." The older lady clucked and her salt-and-pepper beehive hairdo wiggled. "I haven't seen you in a week."

"Well, my mom came to visit."

"That's wonderful."

"And I've been cleaning out the attic."

"Settling in. Good for you." Lorma patted her arm. "I want you to come for dinner tonight."

"Oh, I don't know."

"Yes, I insist. And bring your pup."

Lydia envisioned Gideon storming through the door, ready to pummel her sweet, quickly growing ball of fur. The same sweet thing that had chewed a hole in the carpet in the bedroom. The carpet, of all things. Thankfully, it had been in a perfect spot for an end table.

"I won't take no for an answer." Lorma lifted her eyebrows.

"Okay. What should I bring?"

"How 'bout one of your pies? I've had a hankering for another taste all week. You really should think of selling them."

Lydia's heart swelled to the point she thought it might burst. *The third person to say that this week.* Maybe God had a plan with her pies. She'd keep her eyes and ears open to what He showed her. Excitement welled inside her, not just at the thought of selling pies but also at the thought of totally surrendering every aspect of her life to God.

"I better get to the car before my ice cream melts." Lorma walked away with a wave. "I'll see you tonight. Five o'clock."

"Okay. Thanks, Lorma."

Lydia headed into the store. The drummer's rat-a-tat grew stronger. Oh, how she missed the coffeehouse she used to go to in Indianapolis. The quaint shop sold the best scones and muffins and the most delicious coffee. A sigh escaped her lips as she thought about it.

"Not feeling too well today?" the woman behind the deli asked.

Lydia forced a smile. "I'm fine. I just haven't had my

morning coffee, and my head is throbbing."

"I understand that. My husband's job was relocated, but when we lived in Muncie, I used to visit the neatest coffee shop at least three times per week. This place was really unique; it was actually in a lady's home. A really nice old Victorian-type house. . ."

The woman continued to chatter for several minutes longer. The pounding in Lydia's brain grew louder, and she could focus on nothing except coming up with a polite way to end the conversation.

". . .and the woman who owned the place made the most amazing pies."

Lydia perked up, forcing the drummer to take a moment's reprieve. "Really?"

"Oh, yes."

"I really miss that coffee shop." The woman wiped her gloved hands against her apron front. "Oh well. Is there anything I can get for you?"

Lydia got some chicken and tuna fish salads then continued on her way through the store. The woman's words replayed in Lydia's mind. *God, could this be something I could do? Show me, Lord.*

After grabbing her final item, a gallon of milk, Lydia headed for the checkout aisle.

"Ouch."

Lydia gasped as she pulled her cart away from a pair of well-worn jeans. "I'm so sorry." She looked up.

It was Gideon.

Of course.

❧

"Hello, Lydia." Gideon couldn't help but take in the oversized polka-dot-and-striped pants and not-so-matching T-shirt. To anyone else, she must have appeared worse than what the cat dragged in, as Mama always said when his sisters tried to wear the grunge look to school. To him, she looked adorable.

"Oh, hey." She pushed a curl behind her ear. Another endearing motion he'd noticed she did quite often.

"Getting some groceries, I see."

"A few." Lydia picked up a scandal magazine, opened it, gasped, and put it back on the rack.

He could tell she tried to avoid talking to him. No doubt because she probably *had* just rolled out of bed. He had to bite back a chuckle. He never knew what to expect from Lydia. She was totally different from any woman he'd ever met. She was completely Lydia, and no one else.

"Did you have a good visit with your mom?"

She looked at her nails. "It was fine."

"Good. I take it for granted that I get to see my mom every day."

She nodded. She still wouldn't look at him. He found her enchanting, over-the-top endearing. He just wanted to scoop her up and tickle a hearty laugh out of her. Why tickle her, he wasn't sure, but that's exactly what he wanted to do.

"Did you find them okay?" Maria's voice interrupted his thoughts.

Gideon looked toward the entrance to the store and nodded. With his peripheral vision, he noticed Lydia saw Maria, as well.

"You've been in here awhile." Maria's eyes still flitted with anxiousness from the last few hours they'd spent at the hospital. Despite the need of twenty stitches in his thumb, the doctor assured them Jeremy had *luckily* missed the nerves and wouldn't need surgery. Gideon called *luck* by the name of

God. Maria glanced back out the door. "I just wasn't sure if you knew where to look."

"I got 'em." Gideon held up the package of Spiderman Band-Aids.

"Okay, I'm going back to the car with the boys." Maria waved and walked out of the store.

Gideon looked back at Lydia. A stunned expression wrapped her face. She almost appeared hurt. "Her dad works for me. Her son was hurt. I had to take him to the hospital."

She nodded, but her demeanor had changed.

Once again, Gideon felt like a heel. He knew Lydia thought there was something between him and Maria. Really, there wasn't, but he just couldn't decide if there should be. It was Lydia who made his heart beat faster, Lydia who put a smile on his face. But Maria needed him. Kelbe and Jeremy needed a dad. Jim had always been good to Gideon, and the older man remained convinced that God had Gideon picked out as Maria's next husband. In truth, if Lydia hadn't moved to Danville, Gideon probably would have started dating Maria. She was a really nice Christian lady with great kids. But was she what Gideon wanted?

Maybe I'm just a selfish man. Scripture tells us to take care of widows and those less fortunate.

A slight tightness formed in his heart. *Remember Mama's CD. Look at Galatians.*

Show me, God.

A peace settled in his spirit as a scripture floated through his mind. God was talking to Moses when he feared going back to Egypt. Moses didn't know what to say as to who sent him. "I am who I am," God answered. Without a doubt in his heart, Gideon knew "I am" would guide him to a right decision.

five

Lydia rolled the dough Lorma had made from scratch for the dumplings. Lorma stood over the sink picking chunks of meat off the cooked chicken. Rolling the pin over the dough one last time, Lydia knew it was smooth enough to cut noodles, but she wasn't sure of the necessary consistency for dumpling dough. "My grandma used to make chicken and noodles, but I've never had chicken and dumplings."

Lorma looked at the dough on the table. "Fold it up and roll it back out a couple more times, if you don't mind."

"Okay." Lydia began to do as she was told.

"Dumplings are what we always made back in Pike County. You can make them from canned biscuits or Bisquick, but I always like to make them myself." She turned and winked. "Gideon likes them that way."

Warmth flooded Lydia's face, and she brushed the back of her hand against one cheek in an attempt to hide the blush she knew had formed. "I don't know where Pike County is."

"Eastern Kentucky."

"My sister and her family live in Kentucky."

"Really. Where about?"

"Lawrenceburg. She has her own dental practice."

"Well, Pike County's a good ways southeast of your sister." Lorma stopped picking at the chicken and looked outside the kitchen window. "I'd love for you to meet our family."

"I would, too. You have seven kids. . ."

"Eight. My oldest, Sabrina, has three boys. All almost grown. My next girl, Natalie, has three girls. Kylie's after that with an adopted boy and girl and a biological daughter. Amanda's taken over the group with a set of twin boys and five girls. My first son, Dalton, has four sons and a daughter. Gideon's next. Of course you know he doesn't have any children. Then there are my twins, Cameron and Chloe. Chloe's been married a little over a year; no children yet. Cameron, like Gideon, still hasn't found his bride."

"Wow." Lydia held both hands in the air trying to count her fingers. "I lost count of your grandchildren."

"Twenty-one grandchildren all together—ten boys and eleven girls. And I still have three children who don't have any." Lorma clicked her tongue. "The Lord sure has blessed us."

"Can you imagine all those people on this farm?" Lydia envisioned Gideon the first time she met him, when he was mad at George for making a mess. She couldn't even wrap her mind around the chaos of twenty-one children, and she hadn't done the math to figure out how many adults were in that combination Lorma spoke of.

"It's pure heaven. They're coming for the Fourth of July. You'll have to come eat with us and watch the fireworks. My boys put on quite a display."

"I'd love to." Lydia giggled, as heaven was not the scenario her mind had created. Remembering Gideon's response to her puppy ruining his peaches, Lydia wondered what Gideon acted like when his family came to visit. "So, do they all live in Pike County?"

"Oh, no, we moved from there years and years ago. Five of my kids live in southern Indiana. Chloe and Cameron live in Muncie, and of course, Gideon lives here in Danville. Enough about my brood." Lorma washed her hands then wiped them on a dish towel. She sat beside Lydia at the table, pulled off a piece of the dough, and rolled it between her palms. "Like this." She placed the ball on flour-covered wax paper. "Tell me about this coffee and pie shop idea."

Lydia's heart beat faster with excitement. "It's still a rough idea. Maybe you can help me with some of the kinks. I thought of sectioning off part of Grandma's house and making it a coffee room of sorts. I could sell different coffees and make homemade pies."

"Hmm. Who would want to come? Who are you really gearing your place to suit?"

Lydia hadn't thought of that. Who was she targeting? Well, people her age loved to go to coffee shops to socialize with friends and work on assignments for college. But she also wanted to open her shop up to senior ladies who wanted to spend time together. Maybe mothers who needed a few hours without the kids. Hmm. It proved a lot to think about.

"Do you want to focus mainly on women, or men, too? How will you fund opening it? What long-range plans do you have?"

Lorma's questions swirled inside Lydia's head. So much to think about. She needed a pad and pen to jot down some ideas. Needed to find out where to go for financial numbers. How would she plan?

"Lorma, will you help me?"

The older woman's eyes twinkled, and the crow's-feet on their outer side seemed to dance when she smiled. "I'd love to help you." She leaned over the table. "I took some business classes at a tech school right after Richard passed away. My kids didn't know about it." She giggled like a schoolgirl. "I'd love the opportunity to put some of that knowledge to work."

"Perfect, I—"

"And your pies. You've got to make those scrumptious apple pies as the shop's specialty."

Lydia sat back, relishing Lorma's excitement. God was already confirming what He had in mind for her life.

≈

God's not showing me anything. Gideon kicked a small branch across one of the orchard's paths. His trees were doing beautifully. The weather had been exceptional for apple growing; even his peach trees had produced better than he'd anticipated. The treatments had taken well; no signs of disease or insect infestation. This year would probably be the best ever in terms of his crops.

So far it had been the worst in terms of his personal life.

He was sick to death of listening to Jim hint about Maria's need for a husband. He'd become equally disgusted that no matter how much time he spent with the woman, no matter how many times he witnessed her kindness toward her children, him, and his mother, he still had no feelings for her whatsoever.

Several times he'd reconciled himself to forging ahead and talking with Maria, dismissing the way he felt completely. After all, didn't the Bible say the heart is deceitful above all things? Then Lydia's face would pop into his mind, and he'd be flustered like an old mother hen all over again.

If only that woman had stayed in Indianapolis.

Maybe that was the answer to his qualms. He just needed to keep himself good and aggravated with her. Then he wouldn't think about her sky blue eyes and never-ending, ripened-peach-colored curls.

Stop it, man. He pulled a partially broken twig off a nearby tree and tossed it to the ground. That kind of thinking was not going to help him.

Walking toward the house, he spotted George. The scamp was digging a hole the size of the Grand Canyon beside the shed. A perfect hole for Gideon to step into and break his leg when he tried to get out the weed trimmer. Great, Lydia was visiting.

Well, it appears she hasn't looked at the books I bought her. Gideon snapped his fingers, and the pup looked up at him. George's tail wagged rapidly as he raced toward Gideon. *That's a good idea. If I stay aggravated with her, maybe I'll get her off my mind.* He scooped the dog into his hand and bounded toward the house. After hooking George's collar back on the leash, he stomped the dirt off his boots. Determined to see Lydia as just a pretty woman who'd become a friend to his mom, he pushed open the front door.

Lydia was rolling dumplings beside his mother. The light from the kitchen window shone around her, making her look like an angel delivered from heaven to grace his kitchen.

He growled. *Yeah, she's just a pretty woman. Nothing more.*

❧

Lydia sucked in her breath when Gideon walked into the kitchen. She hadn't meant to. In truth, she didn't know why the man had such an effect on her. His hair lay in a mess on top of his head. His stubble, definitely more than a day old, practically covered his cheeks and chin, even his throat. He'd look like a burly mountain man if it weren't for the fact he was actually quite lean in his build, except for his broad shoulders. She squinted, trying to decipher how his eyes looked today.

Realizing he knew exactly what she was doing, Lydia

averted her gaze back to the dumplings and puckered her lips. With terrific effort, she managed not to rebuke herself out loud, but she had no idea if pink covered her cheeks. It probably did.

"George got off his leash again."

Lydia glanced back at Gideon. He'd turned away from them. His voice sounded gruff, more like it had the first day she'd met him. Obviously, he didn't like her dog. Either that or he found her totally inept at taking care of George. "Sorry." Her voice cracked, and she inwardly berated herself for being so wimpy and so stinking attracted to the grouch.

Gideon opened the refrigerator, grabbed a pop, and then shut the door. "He dug a huge hole in front of my shed."

Lydia stood. "I'll go fix—"

"You just sit right down." Lorma grabbed her hand. "Dogs are supposed to dig holes."

"Still, I'll—"

"Sit."

Lorma pointed to the chair, and Lydia couldn't help but obey. She loved the maternal ways of the older woman. She'd missed them since Grandma died.

"Listen here, my grumpy son." Lorma pointed toward the open chair beside her.

"I'm not grumpy."

"Oh yes, you are," Lorma said. "But that's beside the point. I want to tell you about Lydia's business. We've been planning it all afternoon."

Lydia watched Gideon's eyebrows raise just a hair. He seemed interested in what she planned to do. For some reason, that really pleased her. She listened while Lorma shared the plans they'd made. As discreetly as possible, she watched Gideon's expressions. She wondered what an orchard owner—a man who worked with his hands day in and day out—would think about a quaint little coffee shop.

"I've already told her she can have all the apples she needs free of charge this year." Lorma patted Gideon's hand. "She'll come pick them, of course, but you'll need to haul them over to her house."

Lydia watched as Gideon's eyebrows formed a slight frown. Her heart raced as she imagined his thoughts. She hadn't expected Lorma to offer free apples, and in truth, Lydia had never agreed to take them. She figured she'd pay Gideon when it came time to purchase fruit.

"And she needs the rooms fixed up a bit." Lorma went on. "I told her that I knew you wouldn't mind helping."

Gideon's frown deepened, and he looked down at his hands.

She hadn't requested his help either. That was Lorma's idea. She would never presume upon someone else to do her manual labor for her. If Gideon did help, she intended to pay him. Of course, she wouldn't be able to tell Lorma that.

Gideon cleared his throat. "You shouldn't go offering someone's help when you haven't asked. . ."

Lydia sat up straight in the chair. Hackles raised on the back of her neck. "I think I'll be all right on my own, Lorma." She was not a beggar. She would not force anyone to help her do anything. "And I insist I pay for any apples I need. I can always go to another orchard. . ."

"I'll not hear of it." Lorma placed her hand on her chest. "You are our friend, and we'll do whatever needs to be done to help a friend. Right, Gideon?"

Lydia looked at Gideon. He still stared at his hands. "It's a bad idea."

"You see. . ." Lorma smiled at Lydia then snapped back at Gideon. "What?"

Gideon stood and walked toward the door. "She can have all the apples you want her to have, but it's a bad idea."

"It's not a bad idea." Lorma shook her head, looked at Lydia, and pulled off another piece of dough. "And we'll be glad to help."

Lydia had to force herself not to glare at Gideon. It obviously wasn't settled in his mind. A bad idea, huh? *He thinks I'm incapable. A silly, flighty girl who doesn't have what it takes to be a business owner.* He had no faith in her. He proved no better than her mother. The thought of it weighed down on her chest. Inhaling deeply, she lifted her chin and pulled off another chunk of dough. Well, she didn't need his help. She didn't even need his apples. If it weren't for Lorma, she'd grab her purse and her pup and head out of there.

Why had she ever thought Gideon Andrews attractive to begin with? He was nothing more than an overgrown grump!

six

Pulling off the plastic wrap covering the fireworks his brother-in-law had just given him, Gideon walked into the house. He put the evening's display in a container and snapped the lid. They would stay locked in his room and out of the way of the children until dusk.

Making his way downstairs, he listened to his sisters, Kylie and Sabrina, *oohing* and *aahing* over Lydia's apple pie. He peeked around the corner and saw Mama standing beside Lydia, every bit as proud of the young woman as if she were her own daughter.

Why does Lydia have to be so cute? Maybe he wouldn't be so enamored with her if her curls didn't flow past her shoulders like a waterfall and if her eyes didn't battle the sky on a clear day for beauty.

Sabrina pinched off a piece of Lydia's piecrust and popped it into her mouth. Her eyes widened. "Lydia, you'll make a fortune selling these."

He watched as Lydia's cheeks darkened. Her blushes were almost irresistible to him. Every time pink spread across her face, he itched to kiss its warmth. *And the woman blushes at least once every time I see her.*

"Lorma's planning the shop with me." Lydia pushed a strand of hair behind her ear. "Your mom has a lot of business sense."

Gideon bit back a snort. The shop idea was simply

ludicrous. Danville didn't have a large enough population to support such a shop. How many people would want or have the time to sit in someone's actual house and pay for coffee and pie? It made no sense to him.

But Mama remained all for it. Now, she'd not only invited Lydia to their family Fourth of July supper, but Jim, Maria, and Maria's boys, as well. If he didn't enjoy spending this limited time with his nieces and nephews so much, he'd be upstairs in his room with some kind of stomach bug.

Glancing out the kitchen window, he saw Natalie and her husband and three girls pull into the driveway. An escape. Gideon darted out the back door and ran to his sister's car. He hugged his sister and each of her girls then shook hands with Natalie's husband.

"Are we going to play football?" Natalie's ten-year-old, Tabby, asked.

Gideon leaned down and pinched her chin. "You think you're big enough to take on your Uncle Gideon this year?"

She giggled, stuck out her chin, and nodded her head. "Oh yeah. You're going down this year."

"You and what army's going to get me down?"

"We're the army, Uncle Gideon."

Gideon turned and saw two of Amanda's older girls and Kylie's daughters all racing toward him.

"Get him!" they screamed in unison.

Before Gideon could prepare a defense, the four girls and Tabby jumped on his legs and back. Hands covered his stomach, his shoulders, and his legs in an effort to tackle him. Staying upright appeared the best way to ensure no one was smashed when he fell, but the girls had gotten bigger and stronger over the last year.

"I think they're actually going to get him down!" Natalie's thirteen-year-old, Terri, exclaimed. "I'm in this time."

Gideon took a deep breath and gritted his teeth. Now it was a matter of pride. He couldn't allow his girly nieces to force him to the ground. He'd stand strong no matter how many of them. . .

His foot slid a bit in the dirt.

No problem. With the strength of a determined mule, he slid it back in place.

"Aha, charge!"

This came from one of the nieces who was not currently attached to his body. Another girl who had grown quite considerably in the last year, Gideon noted. One of Amanda's, if he heard the voice correctly.

Before he could analyze further, he felt the impact of the stringy, yet unbelievably strong body hanging from his shoulders on his back. If it was the last thing he did, he would not budge.

A quick peek at the house exposed six women—four sisters, his mother, and Lydia—watching the show. Five of the six were doubled over in laughter. Lydia stood still, gripping the porch post with one hand, the other placed over her heart as if she were saying the pledge of allegiance. The utter shock and wide-eyed expression suggested she had never seen anything like this in her life.

How many girls did he have hanging onto his body? He started to count. Let's see, two clung to one leg. . .

His knee started to give. With more strength than Superman, he popped it back into its straightened position.

One on his other leg. One dangled from his back. Two had wrapped themselves around his waist. Surely, they were uncomfortable. Probably doing more damage to each other than to him.

But Gideon Andrews would not budge.

"This year, Uncle Gideon, you're going down."

Gideon turned and looked eye-to-eye with his oldest niece, fifteen-year-old Tilly. She held his youngest niece, Amanda's poor, innocent two-year-old, on her hip. He glanced beside her. The last three of his nieces—the ones who weren't already attached to his legs—smiled with the most ornery, mischievous smiles he'd ever seen in his life.

"Charge!" Tilly yelled.

This can't be good.

The remaining five joined the six. Girlish squeals sounded all around him. Hands and feet picked and kicked from every angle. Before he had a chance to take another breath, his right foot slipped in the dirt and his left knee buckled.

He hit the ground.

Twenty-two hands, twenty-two feet, and eleven girls jumped off him and into the air in triumph. They had grounded their up-to-now undefeated uncle.

He looked at Lydia and sheepishly shrugged his shoulders. "First year they got me."

❧

Lydia had never seen so many people climb on one person in her life. The grin that never left Gideon's face was proof of his love for those girls. The women around her burst into cheers when Gideon hit the ground. A bit hard, she feared, but no one seemed distressed, so she didn't say anything.

"That was worth the drive." The last sister to arrive handed a casserole dish to Kylie and kissed Lorma on the cheek.

Lorma turned to Lydia. "Lydia, this is Natalie. Natalie, Lydia."

Lydia shook hands with the woman. All of Gideon's sisters were exceptionally attractive. Lydia, with her face splattered with an innumerable number of freckles, felt yet another moment of self-consciousness.

"It's so good to finally meet you." Natalie wrapped her arms around Lydia. "Mama's talked nonstop about you every time I call. It's about time I can put a face to the name."

Lydia forced her mouth to grin. This family proved amazingly kind, but just as amazingly overwhelming. Never in her life had she been around so many people, especially so many children. Mother's incessant manners kicked in, and Lydia found her tongue. "I'm happy to meet you, as well."

Natalie studied her for a moment. Lydia pushed a stray hair away from her face and noted an ant crawling up the porch post.

"Overwhelming, huh?" Natalie's voice stayed low enough that only Lydia heard her.

Lydia looked back up at the woman she knew had to be more than a decade older than herself, and still Natalie looked as if she'd just finished college. "In a good way."

Natalie wrapped her arm around Lydia's shoulder and squeezed. "Definitely in a good way. You'll miss us before you know it."

Warmth washed through Lydia as she realized this family exuded everything she'd wanted growing up. She'd experienced a good deal of love and acceptance with Grandma, but her mom and sister. . . Well, Lydia was just never as "good" at things as they were.

When Allison tried out for cheerleading, she'd not only made the team, she'd become captain. When she joined the Students Against Drunk Driving club, she'd become the president. When she'd gone to college, she'd made a 4.0, even tested out of her first biology class.

Mom was even more distinguished. Top lawyer in her firm. Running for state office. There was no doubt in Lydia's mind she'd win. On top of her career, she'd been PTA Treasurer, an author of a self-help book, and more.

Lydia could not keep up. Deep down, she'd never really even wanted to.

Looking at all Gideon had been blessed with in his life and having discovered Christ as a personal Savior and intimate friend, she wanted contentment and peace—the kind only He could give—and quietness and assurance that could only be found when she spent time with her Father.

The world looked so different. She watched as a good bunch of the children played football. One of the older girls held the youngest boy, handing him an animal cracker with a free hand. Two of the smaller boys chased a bug of some kind in the grass. Most of the men stood beside the shed talking. She looked in the door at most of the women bustling over the food.

This family seemed different, too, and she was excited to get to know them.

She looked back into the yard. Gideon held a small boy in his arms. The dark-haired child couldn't have been more than three. An older version of the boy stood beside Gideon, holding onto Gideon's pant loop. The gorgeous woman from the store stood just a few feet in front of him.

Embarrassed to be staring but unable to look away, Lydia watched as the smaller boy held up his thumb in front of Gideon's face. Gideon grimaced as he kissed the boy's bandaged finger. The older boy said something, and Gideon looked down at him and smiled.

Something flew near the woman's face. She swatted it away. Even when she scrunched her face at the insect, she still looked beautiful. The bug flew toward Gideon and the smaller boy. The boy squirmed in Gideon's hand, but Gideon held him tight. The woman swatted the bug away from Gideon's hair above his ear.

She swatted again, and Lydia felt her heart collapse into her stomach.

"She's quite a beautiful woman."

Lydia gasped and placed her hand on her chest. She smiled at Gideon's youngest sister, Chloe. "You scared me."

Chloe nodded toward the woman. "Her name is Maria. She's a widow."

Lydia tried to look around at the other people playing and talking in the yard. They seemed to blur together, and Lydia willed herself not to shed a single tear at this happy gathering.

Chloe continued. "I think her mother was a catalog model when she was young." Chloe pointed to the men in front of the shed. "Jim, Maria's dad, he's one of Gideon's workers. He and his wife sure did have some really beautiful kids. I've seen pictures of Maria's sister. . .before she passed away in a car accident."

Lydia frowned and looked Chloe in the eye. "That must have been terrible for them."

"Yeah. Maria was pretty young, if I'm remembering right." Chloe looked up at the sky. "It's going to be a beautiful night. Perfect for fireworks."

Lydia gazed at the heavens. The sky was gorgeous—shades of blue and purple hung toward the ground while veins of pink and white adorned the middle. As Lydia lifted her eyes all the way above her head, she noted the mild blue above her. A single star dotted the sky as well as the white tracks of an aircraft of some kind. "You're right."

"You wouldn't know this, but I know my brothers better than any of my sisters do."

Lydia tore her gaze from God's natural beauty and looked back at the woman she'd met only hours before. "What?"

"You see, my parents had my four sisters, two of my brothers, then me and Cameron. Well, the girls never wanted to play with the little baby, so I always ended up with the boys."

"I see." Lydia nodded her head, but she had no idea why Chloe was telling her this.

"Since I always had to tag along with the boys, I became quite a tomboy. Got to the point where none of them could beat me at soccer, and I was a great opponent to practice with at any of their other sports." She leaned closer. "Even though they did usually beat me."

Lydia furrowed her brows. She had no idea where any of this was going. She could tell the women were doing a lot of moving in the kitchen, and Lydia hated not to help out the very first day she met them. The last thing she wanted was for Lorma and her daughters to think Lydia wasn't willing to help.

"He doesn't care about her."

"What?" Lydia stared at Chloe. "Who doesn't care about who?"

Chloe pointed at Gideon. "He may *want* to care about her. Gideon is about the kindest, sweetest guy on the planet, but Maria is not the woman he's after."

"It makes no difference to me." Lydia shifted her weight

and crossed her arms in front of her chest. "I'm here because your mom is my friend. It's got nothing to do with Gideon."

"That's too bad." Chloe kicked a rock off the porch. "'Cause you're the one he cares about." She leaned close and whispered. "He's just not ready to admit it yet."

Lydia looked back at Gideon, Maria, and the boys. The scene was endearing, a perfect Norman Rockwell picture. They looked like the cutest family ever. It made Lydia sick to her stomach, but how could Chloe get "he likes you" out of the scene that Lydia was seeing.

"Hey, can you keep a secret?" Chloe stepped closer. "After the fireworks, I'm going to tell the family I'm expecting. You'll get to see Mama flip."

Lydia hugged her new friend and watched as she escaped into the house. For the briefest of moments, Lydia glanced back at Gideon. He looked up at her and smiled. Her heart sped as she turned and moved back into the kitchen. If only Chloe knew him as well now as she did when they were kids. Lydia had a feeling a lot had changed since Chloe had the inside scoop.

seven

Gideon hefted the box containing the metal utility shelves and placed it in the shopping cart. He rubbed his aching forearms. The load had been heavier than he'd anticipated.

"Let's see." Maria bent over the cart and read the side of the box. "It says we need a Phillips screwdriver. I'm not sure if I have one."

"I do. We'll run by my house and get it before heading over to your apartment."

Maria blinked, causing long lashes to swipe her cheek. Her smile remained sincere, yet purposeful in a way he didn't like. "I really appreciate your help." She touched the top of his hand, and he politely pulled away, shoving it in his front pocket. "I know Dad can be. . ."

Gideon couldn't help but inhale a long breath at the mention of Maria's dad. Jim had practically insisted Gideon help Maria pick up utility shelves for her apartment. Supposedly, his worker had come down with some kind of illness, even though he was as healthy as a fresh-picked apple the day before.

In truth, Gideon didn't mind helping Maria. But now she was putting pressure on him. Her stance had changed, and Gideon knew Jim was no longer the only one who wanted a ring on Gideon's finger.

"Gideon."

Gideon snapped from his thoughts and looked at Maria.

Both hands were planted firmly on her hips. *I have got to start paying better attention.* "Sorry, did you say something?"

"I *said* we'll need to get a move on because Dad needs me to pick up the boys by five."

That was another thing that grated on Gideon's nerves. Jim felt too sick to help his daughter but well enough to care for two rambunctious boys. It was one thing to help Maria; it was another to be made to feel guilty for having not married her yet. And Gideon had just about had enough.

He might even be able to form feelings for her if he felt he could do it on his own. Widows should be cared for, the Bible said so specifically, but Gideon was still a man, and he still wanted to be the one pursuing a relationship.

"Gideon!"

A familiar voice sounded from the back of the store. He turned and saw his mother pushing a cart toward them. Her high bun shifted left to right with each step. A smile lit her face as she peered over the rim of her glasses at him.

Wearing a pair of athletic capris and matching T-shirt, Lydia walked beside her. She gave a quick wave then looked back at the slips of paper in her hands. Curls framed her face as she had her hair in two long pigtails. He hadn't seen anyone's hair fixed like that since he was a young teen. Lydia looked every bit like a young, bubbly girl.

He chewed on the inside of his mouth. *She's the reason I'm having trouble forming feelings for Maria.* "What are you doing here?" Gideon asked. Out of the corner of his eye, he noticed Maria's demeanor and expression had changed in a way he'd never seen before. The woman looked like a mountain lion ready to attack at a moment's provocation.

"We're picking out colors for the coffee room." Mama pointed to the color swatches Lydia held. "She's pretty sure she wants to go with a warm—"

"You're still thinking about that?" Gideon looked from his mother to Lydia.

"Yes." Lydia seemed to have stood up a bit more, and she focused fully on him.

"Have you talked to anyone about cost, about interest, anything? You know starting a business is not as easy—"

"Thank you for your concern." Lydia looked at his mother. "But Lorma and I have done a lot of research and—"

"Gideon is right." Maria's voice sounded more like a purr. Gideon glanced toward her and realized she'd nudged her way closer to him. "He knows a lot more about these—"

"Hogwash." Mama swatted the air. "Gideon doesn't know the research we've done." She grabbed Gideon's arm and pulled him toward her. "Now, we're down to these two colors. Which do you like?"

"Mama, I'm not picking out paint for a coffeehouse that I think you're rushing into." He sneaked a peek at Lydia. Her lips pinched so tight he worried they'd get stuck that way. The glare in her eyes exposed the anger brewing behind them.

He bit back a sigh. He wasn't trying to be discouraging. If they'd give him half a chance, he just wanted to be sure she knew what she was getting into. Opening a business took a lot of work and determination. It took a lot of long-range planning and a willingness to stick with it through the hard times. He studied Lydia for a moment. *I'm just not sure she's thought through the long haul.*

Mama clicked her tongue, forcing him from his thoughts. "Don't be ridiculous. Just choose a color."

Gideon grabbed the color swatches from her hands. "Mama,

you two are moving too fast."

"Excuse me." Lydia took the palettes from him. "It's *my* coffee shop. If you don't want to share a preference, that's fine."

"Have you spoken with anyone besides my mom? What about start-up costs and building permits and—"

"You don't think I'm smart enough to have thought of that?" Mama's expression fell. "You don't know that I took a few business classes after your father passed away."

Now he'd hurt his mother's feelings, and he didn't know she'd attended classes, but they still needed more advice, more guidance. "Mama, I never said you weren't smart. You're one of the most intelligent women I know." The expressions on Mama's and Lydia's faces proved they were done listening. He was making a mess of this.

Mama fidgeted with the front of her sweater. Practically dismissing him, she turned toward Lydia. "Well, he'll still help you paint, Lydia."

"You're helping her paint?" Maria's voice sounded strained, and Gideon turned toward her. A moment of fury flashed across her face and was quickly shaded with a sweet smile. "I love to paint. I'll be glad to help."

Gideon looked back at Lydia, whose face had shifted through various shades of red. He noted the mutilated color swatches in her hands.

"Thank you, but I don't mind doing it myself," Lydia spit through gritted teeth.

Guilt weighed fresh on his heart. He wasn't trying to be an ogre about opening the business; he just knew how hard it was. He'd never had a chance to sit with Lydia and tell her why he was afraid for her to start it. Whether he agreed with it or not, he was willing to help her. "I said I'd help paint, Lydia." He touched her arm and ignored the slight gasp that escaped from Maria. "I will help you."

"Then it's settled." Maria clapped her hands and smiled. "We're having a paint party at Lydia's."

Gideon sighed, wishing he'd be the only one in attendance. He and Lydia needed to talk.

❧

Who did Gideon Andrews think he was? For that matter, who did he think she was? Obviously, he viewed her as incompetent. He proved no better than her mother. At least her mother had known Lydia all her life. She smacked her hand against her kitchen cabinets. This. . .this man was making judgments about her, and he barely knew her.

She grabbed a pop from the refrigerator. Sure, she tended to be a bit on the flighty side. Sitting at the table, she took a drink of the caffeinated beverage. Okay, so she'd had more jobs than she could count on both hands. So she'd taken more classes than the average person with a degree. In truth, she'd taken so many she could have a master's degree if she'd stuck with a single program. She couldn't deny she had no experience running a business and that she relied heavily on the advice of a woman she'd met only weeks before. And if she chose to be honest, she had to acknowledge that she'd spent every penny of the money she'd received from her grandmother's will and still taken out a chunk of the money she'd worked so hard to save over the years.

"Who am I kidding?" She pulled the rubber bands from her hair and raked her fingers through her tangled locks. "This is just another one of Lydia's crazy ideas. Another ridiculous notion at trying to find my niche."

She rested her elbows on the table and peered at the expansive land behind Grandma's house. "Why can't I just be stable? Content?"

Miles of lush green land swayed with the wind beyond her grandmother's expansive flower garden. Wildflowers and various weeds laced the green with purple, yellow, and red. Trees, lush and enormous, stood proudly reaching for the heavens. Some were in clusters, while others made their statements by standing alone. A row of electric poles trailed down the land, and she could see a few homes dotting the distance.

Gideon's orchard, full and healthy, lined the far right. She could see only a small part of it. To her left were rows and rows of corn. Grandma's land fell between the orchard and the corn rows. Beyond the yard, the land hadn't been cultivated. It exhibited the beauty God had originally given it.

Emotion overwhelmed her as scripture she'd read not too long ago flooded her spirit. Jesus had said something about if God could dress the lilies to be as pretty as they were, how much more would He take care of her.

A strong compulsion to be in the very presence of the majesty her God had created spurred Lydia to leave the table and walk out the back door. She strolled past the beauty Grandma had arranged and into the bounty of God's craftsmanship. Inhaling the fresh scent and welcoming the soft kisses of the wind, Lydia lifted her face to the heavens. White clouds spread across the blue as if God were making taffy of them. The day would be exceptionally warm if not for the breeze.

Closing her eyes, she allowed the picture she enjoyed to repaint itself in her mind. "Oh, Jesus." His name slipped from her lips, just above a whisper. Chirping birds and talking insects paid her no mind and continued their communications with one another. "I have no doubt of Your love for me. I have no doubt You will provide for my needs. It's me I doubt."

Tears slipped from her eyes, and she swiped them away with the back of her hand. Opening her eyes again, she noted two birds dancing with one another in the air. They made their way toward a cluster of trees and were soon out of sight.

"But I dwell within You."

The Spirit's soft pricking warmed her heart. "'I can do everything through him who gives me strength.'" The scripture spilled from her lips.

"But is this what I'm supposed to do, Lord? What if I get tired of it?" She gazed back at the heavens. "You know I don't have the best track record when it comes to sticking with what I start."

"But I do."

"'He who began a good work in you will bring it to completion.'" The verse, though not verbatim, slipped through her lips and she smiled. God hadn't spoken to her audibly, but He'd spoken to her heart, and she couldn't deny Him.

Bending down, she snipped several wildflowers from the earth's carpet. Studying the various petals and intricate combinations of colors, she could never doubt that her all-knowing Father took great pride in the intricacies of His works.

And that included her.

He cared about the ins and outs of her life. He cared about her flightiness, about her doubts. He'd formed her just the way He wanted, and He would see her through any task. Day to day. Moment to moment.

Even this.

❧

"We're here."

Lydia barely had time to check her mascara in the mirror before Maria's voice called from the front door. Lydia peeked around the corner, and Maria lifted the paintbrush and pan higher in the air. Maria acted cheerful and anxious to get started, but Lydia couldn't help but wonder if that had more to do with the man standing beside her and less to do with a desire to assist Lydia.

Lydia opened the door for Gideon and Maria. She noted Gideon's stoic silence in direct contrast to Maria's exaggerated praises over the house. Lydia lifted her chin. She didn't need Gideon's approval. It was God she sought to please.

"Which room?" Gideon's noncommittal tone grated even more on Lydia's nerves. No one forced him to help her.

Gazing up at him, she noted the determined gleam in his eye. He wanted to complete the job quickly. Her irritation grew, and she decided not to argue with him about staying. *I won't worry about his attitude. I'll just thank You, God, for the help.*

"The parlor." Lydia pointed toward the kitchen. "It's just to the left of the kitchen."

Before Lydia could shut the door, Maria marched ahead, and Gideon and Lydia followed. Maria stopped just inside the door, and Lydia bumped into Gideon's back.

"Sorry." Lydia looked up at him. His expression softened, and Lydia found herself drowning in the depths of his eyes once again. The contrast of his sun-darkened skin with the lighter, sandy color of his stubble intrigued her. The mystery of their texture made her long to touch them.

"It's a bit small for a coffee shop." Maria snorted. "What do you think, Gideon?"

An icy glare crossed his gaze before he looked away from Lydia and into the parlor. "I have no opinion." He walked past Maria and placed the paint cans on the floor that Lydia had already covered with plastic. "I'm just here to paint."

Fury welled within Lydia. First of all, the room was not small. Second, if it weren't for the fact that she adored his mother, she'd kick him out of her house that very moment. Her attraction to him only made her more furious. She didn't want to touch his stubble; she wanted to yank the hairs off his face. *Okay, that's a bit dramatic, Lydia. Chill out a bit.*

He turned toward her and crossed his arms in front of his chest. "Where do I start?"

Lydia bit her lip. *Chill out a whole big bit.* She willed herself to stay calm and forced a smile to her lips. "Any wall would be fine." She knew her tone betrayed her feelings, but she didn't care. The man had no right to treat her this way.

The colors in Gideon's eyes seemed to swirl together as they had the first day she'd met him—the day he was angry with George. *Good. He can be just as huffy as he wants. Maybe he'll get mad enough he'll go home.*

"Gideon," Maria's sultry voice purred in such an obviously flirtatious way Lydia thought she'd lose her lunch. "I can't pour the paint without making a mess. Will you help me?"

"Sure." Gideon's stance stiffened as he helped Maria with the paint.

Maria touched his arm possessively and glanced back at Lydia. A sly smile bowed her lips. Embarrassed that she'd been watching, Lydia looked away. What did she care if Maria flirted with Gideon? The man was more aggravating than a plantar wart.

She grabbed the other paint can and poured its contents

into a second pan without the aid of the overgrown grump. Lydia had trouble believing Gideon was truly related to her sweet friend, Lorma. The quicker they could get this done, the quicker he and Maria could go home.

❧

The faster we can get this place painted, the faster we can leave. Gideon showed Maria how to use the roller for the third time. For a woman who said she knew how to paint, he sure had to do a lot of assisting. And it was getting on his last nerve.

What had happened to Maria? She used to be sweet and kind. He would have considered her a friend. Since Lydia moved to Danville, Maria had become a madwoman. She showed up at the orchards every day, to dinner almost every other night, and she needed more help fixing little things around her apartment than the place could hold.

Guilt nudged at his heart. Of course Maria needed help. She was a single mom with two active boys. In the past, he'd never once minded helping her. But she had changed. She didn't seem to just want his help. Her intentions had become evident in the last few weeks. What she didn't understand was that Gideon wanted to be the pursuer. He wanted to be able to get his head clear and figure out why Lydia just wouldn't leave his mind. He needed some answers from God, who had become overtly silent.

Gideon dipped his paintbrush back into the pan. Jim had become more insistent, as well. It had gotten to the point that he avoided his employee at all costs. Sometimes Gideon even neglected getting all his work completed.

Maria looked at him and pouted. "I think I need your help again."

Enough was enough. Gideon nodded toward a chair. "Why

don't you take a rest? I really need to finish this."

By the soft gasp from Lydia and the ashen expression that wrapped Maria's face, he knew he had been too curt. Maria blinked several times and placed the roller in the tray. "I'm sor—"

"No, I'm sorry I snapped at you." *A heel. You're an overgrown heel.*

Lydia clapped her hands together. "You know what. I think it's time for a break. I've got some sliced meat in the fridge. Let's eat some lunch." She wrapped her arm around Maria's slouching frame and sneered back at him.

Gideon watched as the two made their way into the kitchen. *God, when did things get so complicated? Why aren't You answering me?*

He watched as Lydia pulled plates out of the dishwasher. She grabbed a loaf of bread off the counter. *It was when she moved here that everything went nuts. One small, pretty woman had turned his world upside down.*

Wiping his hands on his pants, he walked out of the kitchen. Both women looked at him. One in anguish. The other in frustration.

And it's not going to get better any time soon.

eight

Lydia wiped beads of perspiration from her forehead. With the beginning of August in sight, the weather had turned exceptionally hot. Even at midmorning, watering the flower gardens had become a sweaty experience. George, though still every bit the rascal he'd always been, was smart enough to find a lounging spot in the shade.

"I found it." Lorma burst through the back door waving a paper in her hand. George jumped up and raced over to her. "Stay down." She swatted him away. "I knew if I looked long enough I'd find the recipe." Having come over early that morning, Lorma had brought her box of recipes and scoured through the collection for one she wanted Lydia to try baking.

Lydia wiped her hands on the front of her pants. "Let's see it."

"Not with those filthy hands." Lorma held the sheet away from Lydia's grasp. Lydia laughed at how much she felt like one of Lorma's own children. God had given the relationship to Lydia after mourning the death of her grandma, and Lydia relished it. "It's my great-aunt's recipe for apple tarts. Since she passed away, I've never tasted any so good."

Lydia looked at the ingredients and directions, praying she could make them well enough to please her friend. "I'll give it a try."

"I can't wait to taste them." Lorma held the paper to her chest. "Are you almost finished out here? I thought we were going to talk about furniture, too."

Lydia couldn't hold back her chuckle. Her older friend proved every bit as excited about opening the coffee shop as Lydia, and in truth, Lorma had some wonderful ideas. "I am. Let me turn off the water hose."

Once the water stopped, Lydia and George followed Lorma into the parlor of the house. The fresh, spice-colored paint on the walls almost matched the color of the hardwood floors. "I hadn't thought about the floors when I picked out the color," Lydia admitted.

"I think it will look wonderful. You just need to get some darker furniture and pictures with darker frames." Lorma snapped her fingers. "Have you ever thought about putting up chair railing and painting the bottom half a darker color? You know, something the color of rich coffee?"

Lydia nodded her head. "That's a great idea. I think I'll buy some furniture first and see how it looks before I do anything else to the walls."

Lorma winked. "Smart girl. Gilley's Antique Mall has some really nice tables. Some are very original looking. You might be able to find a reasonably priced sofa, as well. I'll call Gideon and see if he can take an early lunch and run you over there."

Panic welled in her heart. The last person she wanted to see was Gideon. She shook her head. "No, no. Don't interrupt him. I can drive myself."

Lorma pulled out her cell phone. "Don't be silly. If you find something you want to buy, you'll need a truck to haul it back in." She lifted her hand. "Gideon, do you have time to take. . ."

Lydia grimaced and motioned toward the bathroom. After making her way to the "purple" room, she shut the door. Peering at her reflection in the mirror, she gripped the sides of the white pedestal sink. She loved Lorma, really, she did, but this whole let's-make-Gideon-and-Lydia-friends thing just wasn't working.

Never in her life had she felt so much aggravation with a man. He didn't support the coffee shop idea at all, yet Lorma continued to push it on him. And Maria? Well, that remained a whole different thing all together. The woman obviously had an attraction to Gideon. Lydia couldn't figure out Gideon's feelings, but she could still tell Maria felt a compulsion of some kind to prove Gideon belonged with her. *Well, she can have him.*

Even as the thought escaped her mind, Lydia sighed at the unmistakable attraction she felt for the man. He treated his mother like a treasure. His willingness to work hard was evident by just a glimpse at his home and orchard. She didn't doubt for a moment that he loved the Lord. *But I get on his nerves, that's for sure.*

A knock sounded at the door. The noise sent George into a chorus of barks. "You okay in there?" Lorma's voice held a hint of concern.

Lydia almost giggled. Lorma definitely treated her as if she were one of her own children. "I'm fine."

"Well, good. Hurry up. Gideon's going to be here in ten minutes."

Lydia gasped as she peered at her reflection. Ten minutes? She hadn't even run a brush through her hair let alone put on any makeup. *I've got to remember to be ready at all times when I'm with Lorma.*

She grabbed an oversized comb from the medicine cabinet and swept it through her curls. She pulled up her sides and bangs and clipped them on top of her head. Remembering the morning at the grocery store, she shrugged. "He's seen me look worse."

۲

Anxious to see Lydia, Gideon looked forward to taking her to Gilley's. Finally, he'd have the chance to talk to her about this business idea. He needed to let her know how hard it would be and how much commitment it would take. *I can't deny I'll enjoy spending a little time with her, as well.*

Mama, though her intentions were good, had never started a business. The two women were excited, but they needed some guidance. They needed to understand that their expectations might take years to come to fruition.

For that matter, Gideon wasn't convinced they ever would. Danville was a small community, and a coffee shop a few miles away from town would have a hard time thriving. People would never just "happen" upon Lydia's shop. They'd have to know about it and drive to her house to frequent it. *She's got to at least listen to me before she takes out any loans.*

Gideon pulled up to Lydia's house. Though he really didn't expect her to find a lot of stuff, he'd hitched the trailer to his truck just in case.

Mama and Lydia were already waiting outside. Lydia's long hair flowed down her back, but a clip held the front away from her face. Her blue eyes seemed to glow in the sunlight, and Gideon, once again, could not deny his attraction to her. No matter how many times he saw her, he never tired of it. At the orchards, at home, at night, he always yearned to see her again.

He jumped out of the cab and walked over to the passenger's side. After opening the door, he motioned inside. "Hop in, ladies."

Mama pointed to Lydia. "You're going to have to get in first. I can't sit on that hump in the middle."

Gideon watched as Lydia's face paled. He could see she hadn't anticipated sitting so close to him.

Mama shooed Lydia toward the door. "And you'll have to take me home before you head into town."

"What?" Gideon and Lydia asked in unison.

Lydia looked up, and her eyes met his for the briefest amount of time before she exhaled and looked away.

"Well, sure. I have to get lunch ready for you and Jim." She nudged Lydia. "Of course, you're invited, too."

Gideon noted Lydia's stance of discomfort and turned toward his mom. "Why don't we all eat at the Mayberry Café?"

Mama's eyebrows met in a frown. "Then who will feed Jim?"

"We can bring something back for him."

"That's silly. I already have leftover soup in the refrigerator. No sense in letting it go to waste. Just take me home."

"But, Lorma, I want you to help me pick out the furniture." Lydia's voice almost sounded like a whine as she hopped into the cab, her hesitance apparent as she scooted to the middle.

"Don't be silly. You've got a great eye." Mama jumped in beside her, knocking Lydia even closer to Gideon's side.

Gideon wanted to groan as he made his way to the driver's side and tried to get in without touching Lydia. An impossible feat. The poor woman sat sandwiched between his mother and him, and if Gideon didn't know any better, he'd believe Mama took up more room than necessary.

The engine growled to a start, and Mama started talking again. Gideon couldn't focus on anything she said. All he could think about was the softness of Lydia's arm rubbing against his. The floral scent of her hair tantalized his nostrils, and not for the first time, he wished he had the right to lean over and inhale his fill of her locks.

He pulled up to his house. Mama jumped out, and Lydia scooted over, all in one motion. "See you two in an hour or so."

Alone in the truck, Gideon contemplated how to approach the coffee shop subject without getting her riled. He didn't want to insult her again. A woman with her feathers ruffled never listened to reason. *Just spit it out.*

He sneaked at peek at her in the passenger's seat. She stared straight ahead. Her nose had the slightest upturn to it. He found it adorable. "Mind if we talk about your coffee shop?"

"Yes."

Gideon furrowed his brows. "Is that 'yes, we can talk about it' or 'yes, I mind.'"

"Yes, I mind."

Gideon gripped the steering wheel. Sneaking another peek, he noticed she still stared straight ahead. *Difficult woman.* "Well, I'd like to have my say just the same."

"Then, by all means."

"Are you being smart?"

Lydia's head snapped toward him. "Am I being smart?" She pointed to her chest. "You did not just say that to me. No one is asking you to help in my endeavor, so why does it matter to you?"

Because I care about you. . .too much. "Not true. Mama's asked me to help several times. Even now I'm helping."

Lydia lifted her finger to make a point then lowered it. "Your mom keeps doing that, and I. . .I don't know how to stop her."

Gideon laughed. "Mama is hard to handle, isn't she?" He pulled into Gilley's parking lot. "I bet this coffee shop is more her idea than yours."

"No, it's mine."

Gideon shut off the engine and turned toward her. "I'm not trying to be a pessimist. I just want to be sure you've checked into if enough people would be interested in a coffee shop. I'd hate for you to take out a loan and get permits if there's not a market. I don't want you to—"

Before he could finish, Lydia opened the door, hopped out, and shut it firmly behind her.

So much for trying to be diplomatic. Gideon grabbed his keys from the ignition and hopped out. She never looked back as he followed her into the antique mall.

They passed row after row of sofas, wingback chairs, and tables. Lydia never said a word.

Hardheaded woman. I wouldn't give her advice now if she paid me. Try to be a friend and she slams the door in a guy's face.

They passed a deep brown love seat that would look nice in the room.

I'm not even going to point that out to her. And I'm not going to help her discuss any prices either. Let her pay too much for all I care.

"I'm ready." Lydia headed toward the checkout desk.

"Didn't find anything you like?"

Lydia glared up at him. "No, I found some things." She smiled at the clerk. "I'd like to purchase the brown sofa, the two red wingback chairs, and both of the black breakfast tables and chairs. I'm fine with the total ticket price"—Lydia pointed toward another section—"if it also includes the throw pillows and the matching three-piece lighting set."

In Pursuit of Peace 83

The clerk studied the total, chewing on her bottom lip. "You've added an awful lot of stuff to that."

"True. But the price shows I've purchased a substantial amount of furnishings."

The clerk thought another moment. "All right. Go get what you want."

As he and the clerk's teenage son packed one item after another out of the antique mall, Gideon still couldn't believe how well Lydia had negotiated. The clerk even threw in a few knickknacks for decorations.

Maybe there was more to Lydia than he realized.

Before he could ponder the notion, his cell phone rang. It was Mama.

ঝ

Lydia still fumed. How much audacity did the man contain? She told him she didn't want to discuss her business with him, yet he wouldn't listen. He acted as if she were a child—an incompetent child. Quite frankly, she got enough of that from her mother.

And who told him she was taking out a loan? No one. Which is why he didn't know that she wasn't borrowing any money.

"That was Mama." Gideon clicked his cell phone shut. "Apparently, she spilled our lunch."

"What? Is she hurt?"

Gideon shook his head. "Apparently, she tripped on the mat and spilled soup all over the floor."

"What a mess. I hate it when I do stuff like that."

Gideon lifted one eyebrow, and Lydia inwardly reprimanded herself. He already thought her incapable. She had no desire to give him more ammunition.

"She said for me to take you to the Mayberry Café."

"Oh, no." Lydia shook her head. "Just take me on home."

Gideon didn't say anything for several moments. Finally, Lydia peeked at him and found him staring at her. "You did really good back there."

Heat rushed to her cheeks. Though he didn't say it, she knew he meant her dealings at Gilley's. Swallowing hard, she willed her face not to darken. "Thanks."

"Let me take you to the café."

"No. It's fine. I have a lot to do at home."

"Okay, the truth is Mama said if I came home and hadn't treated you she wouldn't feed me for a week."

Lydia giggled, knowing Lorma had said just that. If she didn't know any better, she would believe the older woman was trying to fix them up. Lydia shook her head. Lorma remained just a sweet woman with a heart of gold. She didn't see Lydia as daughter-in-law material. The woman had simply adopted Lydia.

"Okay, but let it be known that I had mercy on you even though all you've wanted to do is lecture me." Lydia scrunched her nose. She didn't have to say the last part. Now he'd start in on her all over again.

"I really wasn't trying to stop you from opening the business. I just don't want to see you get hurt."

"Why?"

"I guess. . .I guess I care about you."

If Gideon cared about her, he had a funny way of showing it. Maybe it was a brotherly care. *Or maybe. . .* She shook her head. There could be no possible way the man cared for her in the manner her heart wanted. Besides, she'd spent the last several weeks trying to beat some sense into the obstinate organ.

nine

Bone tired, physically and mentally, Gideon grabbed his Bible and headed for the orchard. He'd been wrestling with God for weeks over Maria and Lydia. It proved silly really, because Lydia had made it apparent she was most definitely not interested.

He trudged toward his favorite tree. Looking down at its trunk, he noted his body seemed to have imprinted itself in the worn base. Gideon found himself more comfortable leaning against that tree than sitting in most chairs.

He touched one of the small apples hanging from a branch. In just over a month, the tree would be filled with lush fruit. By its size and appearance, Gideon expected to have a good year. Economically, this year, it appeared, would be his best.

Yet he felt so disconnected from God.

He lowered himself to his favorite spot and rested the Bible against his chest. Allowing the summer's warm breeze to sweep over him, he watched a bee buzz from one clover to the next. He allowed the serenity of God's creation to wrap him in its soft embrace. It had been too long since he'd sat silently and listened for God.

Maybe that explained His silence.

Closing his eyes, Gideon tried to clear his mind of all his questions. Memories from long ago washed over him. Sitting beside Pa at church when he'd gotten caught talking. The smell of Mama's coffee long before the sun rose. Chasing his sisters with worms in each hand.

His thoughts shifted to the day he'd asked Jesus into his heart. The day he asked God to keep Pa alive through Thanksgiving. The day he asked God to take care of Mama now that she was alone on Earth.

How he wanted what Pa and Mama had. A year ago, he would have never even considered marriage. He wasn't opposed to it; he just wasn't all that interested either. Now all he could think about was Maria and Lydia.

To be honest, he only thought of Lydia.

But duty called him to Maria. Maria made more sense. She was a widowed Christian with two children. She wanted a husband, and she'd make a terrific, doting wife. There was no reason for Gideon not to ask Maria to marry him today.

Except one—Lydia.

Gideon growled. The whole thing was useless. He needed to quit overanalyzing everything and simply refer to God's Word. He opened his Bible.

"Well, there you are."

Gideon looked up. "Cameron, is that you?"

"Yep. I've been looking all over for you."

Gideon stood and hugged his little brother, who now stood every bit as tall and broad as him. "What's going on?"

"I just stopped by to see my mom and big brother."

Gideon studied the younger man. "You drove over an hour just to stop by?"

"Okay, I may have had a bit of a reason, but you have to come to the house so I can show you."

Gideon's curiosity piqued. "Show me?"

"Yep."

Gideon followed Cameron back. Long before they reached

the house, Gideon noticed Mama and another woman on the porch. The woman didn't look familiar, young with long dark hair, and Gideon couldn't make out who she was. Realization dawned. "Is she your reason?"

Cameron smiled and gestured Gideon to hurry. He reached the porch and grabbed the woman's hand, helping her to her feet. "Gideon, allow me to introduce you to my fiancée, Caitlyn."

"Cameron and Caitlyn. . ." Mama chuckled. "Isn't that the cutest thing you've ever heard?"

The young woman's cheeks flamed red at his mother's words, but Gideon noted Caitlyn's gaze never left his brother's face. She looked as tiny as one of those teacups he'd watched Lydia buy for her coffee shop.

A mixture of happiness and envy enveloped Gideon as he extended his hand. A slightly nervous giggle escaped when she touched it. Gideon remained speechless as he shook his soon-to-be sister-in-law's hand. Though he tried to push away the jealous feelings that warred to overtake his happiness for his brother, all Gideon could think about was being the last in his family without a mate.

❧

Lydia pulled the apple tarts out of the oven. The inspector would arrive first thing the next morning for final approval of her business license. She'd been a bundle of nerves the whole day, so she'd decided to try her hand at Lorma's great-aunt's tarts. The first two times she'd tried baking them, they hadn't turned out as Lydia hoped. She made a couple of minor adjustments to the recipe before trying it again. *Third time's a charm, I hope.*

The warm, sweet aroma filled the kitchen, and Lydia's

stomach growled. Her nerves had kept her from eating much. Now her stomach protested. She touched the top of a tart to check for flakiness. A bit of the apple filling burned her finger. Pulling her hand away quickly, she popped the injured finger in her mouth and raced to the sink. She placed the appendage under cold water for several seconds. The burn was small but stung miserably.

She turned off the cold water and reached for a clean cloth so she could wrap up her hand. The water dripped. She was pretty sure she had some aloe vera gel somewhere in the house; she'd just have to think of where. The water dripped again.

She grabbed the faucet knob and turned it all the way off. A steady stream poured. "What in the world?" She tried turning it the other way; the water simply poured harder.

"Oh no." She twisted the knob left and right, right and left. No matter where she tried to stop, the water still dripped.

"Why today?" She tried twisting it one more time with all the strength she could muster. The stream quickened again, and this time she'd tightened it so well she couldn't move it left or right.

"It's Sunday. No plumber's open on Sunday." Panic welled in her heart as she opened the bottom cabinet. The pipes looked fine. Of course, she didn't really know what "fine" was when it came to pipes. The stream continued to flow steadily. "God, what will I do? I'll never pass inspection." She placed her finger under the flow. "I'll never be able to pay the water bill."

Gideon drifted into her mind, and she knew she had no choice but to call him. She'd no sooner hung up the phone with Lorma than her mother called.

"How are things going?" Her mother's voice simpered through the line.

"My final inspection is tomorrow, and the kitchen sink is leaking." As soon as the words left Lydia's mouth, she knew she'd made a mistake.

"Why are Mother's pipes leaking?"

"Mom, I didn't do it on purpose." Lydia was tired of being on the defensive with her mother. She wanted once, just once, for her mother to be proud of her and excited about what she was doing.

"Who'd you call to fix it?" Rita's voice was curt.

"My friend. . .Gideon." Lydia wasn't sure she considered Gideon her friend, but what else would she consider him?

"You've mentioned him a lot. Are you two an item?"

"No!" Lydia tried to keep from screaming into the phone. "Look, Gideon's here. I've gotta go. Bye."

Before her mother could respond, Lydia hung up the phone and opened the door for Gideon. "It's the one in the kitchen."

"Are you okay?"

"Yes. Yes." Her words came out choppy. Anxiety swirled in her empty stomach, making her nauseated. Emotion pounded her head, and she feared at any moment she'd break down into tears.

"Are you sure?"

"Please." Her voice cracked, and Lydia cleared her throat. "Please fix the sink."

Gideon turned off the water to the house and within a matter of moments had changed a gasket of some kind, turned the water back on, and stopped the leak.

"See, nothing to it." Gideon walked toward her. He brushed

her cheek with the back of his hand. "You look pale. Do you feel sick?"

The gentle caress and the strength and warmth of his hand broke the wall within her that she tried so hard to keep intact. Tears, one after the other, raced each other down both cheeks.

"Lydia." Gideon's voice, soft and kind, erupted another wave of emotion. Her chest heaved, and he wrapped his strong, protective arms around her.

She couldn't move. Didn't want to move. She'd never been so out of control, so in need of someone to hold her.

"It's okay." He brushed her hair with his hand and tightened his hold. "It's okay."

The fear of not passing the inspection, the hurt of her mother's continued lack of approval, the confusion of her feelings for the man who held her close weighed so heavy she wrapped her arms around him. Relishing his smell, his tenderness, his strength, she closed her eyes and allowed this moment of comfort.

Her breathing slowed, and she looked up at the man she'd been trying so hard not to love. "Thank you, Gid—"

His lips crashed down on hers with an intensity she'd never known. Every nerve awakened as she accepted his kiss. After what seemed an eternity of bliss, he pulled away, whispering something about care and forever.

All Lydia could think about was the feel of his lips—strong and masculine yet soft and tender—against hers.

28

If Gideon lived to be one hundred, he'd never forget the softness of her lips. He'd never felt so needed and never had such a desire to provide for the need. He'd told her he would care for her forever. And he'd spoken the truth.

Few things in his life had been clearer to him. Just as John said in the Bible, the truth had set him free. Without a doubt, the truth was he'd fallen in love with Lydia.

ten

Gideon sipped his coffee, remembering the sweetness of Lydia's touch and how she fit perfectly in his arms. It hurt him to see her crying, but it felt right to be the one to comfort her pain. He wanted to protect her, to make her happy. For the first time in his life, he longed to love a woman in the manner God spoke of in scripture—more than his own life.

The reality of the depth of his feelings struck him, and he took another sip. Did every man feel as though he could take on the world when the woman he loved was in pain? As she cried in his arms, Gideon would have done anything to make her happy and content. *I've never felt this way, Lord.*

"You're awfully quiet this morning." Mama traced the top of her coffee mug with her finger.

"Just thinking."

"Penny for your thoughts."

Gideon looked at Mama and smiled at her grin. He couldn't even begin to count the many times he'd heard Mama say that. Usually to one of his sisters. They always seemed to be the ones to do the extra thinking. Gideon and his brothers were doers. They rarely worried about anything. "I'm not sure if you can help me."

"Son, I've lived a long time. My guess is I can help you, but if I can't, I know someone who can."

Gideon loved his mother. She drove him to insanity at times, but she truly was a woman of strength and faith. He should have talked to her long ago. "What happens when what you want conflicts with what someone else needs?"

Mama tapped her fingers on the table. "Well, that depends. If you're talking about buying an expensive car just because you think you look good in it and you take on more debt than you can afford. . .well, you better not be buying that car." Mama clicked her tongue. "Or if you're talking about going to an Indianapolis Colts game because you were given free tickets but it's at the same time as your family's annual reunion. . .you better give up those tickets." Mama leaned forward and rested her elbows on the table. "But I don't think those scenarios are what we're talking about."

Gideon shook his head.

"Well, I think a person has to evaluate if he understands need from want."

"Of course I understand need from want." Gideon sat back in his chair. Mama's intense look made him uncomfortable.

"You sure?"

A car door slammed. Footsteps sounded on the porch. Before Gideon had time to respond, the back door flung open. Maria's eyes were as big as a deer's caught in headlights. "Dad is sick."

"What's wrong?" Mama guided a distraught Maria to a chair. Gideon grabbed a mug and poured some coffee.

Maria shook her head and popped up out of the seat. "He's so pale and tired. He says he can't get up. Not even to come to work."

Gideon's concern heightened. Jim never missed work. "Where is he?"

"At his apartment. He told me to go on to work, that he'd be okay." Maria's voice cracked. "I'm scared."

"It's okay, honey." Mama wrapped her arms around her. "Gideon will go get Jim. Where are the boys?"

"At the sitter's. I. . .I didn't want them to see their grandpa. . ." She cried into Mama's embrace. Gideon grabbed his keys and headed out the door.

"Call as soon as you get there," Mama said.

Gideon drove as fast as the law allowed, growing more anxious by the minute. "Lord, Maria needs Jim." Guilt nudged at his heart. If something happened to Jim, Maria wouldn't have anyone. "Please, Lord, help Jim be all right."

He parked the car in Jim's driveway and raced up to the apartment. After pushing the unlocked door open, Gideon saw his employee lying on the couch, pale as bug powder. Jim didn't even respond when Gideon checked his much-too-weak pulse. Gideon lifted him as gently as possible and took him to the truck. "Don't worry, Jim. I'll have you at the hospital in no time."

❧

Lydia opened the door for the inspector. The tall, unbelievably thin, brown-haired man nodded his head. "Morning, ma'am."

"Good morning." Lydia tried not to destroy the hand towel she twisted in her hands. Remembering her manners, she motioned him inside. "I hope you find everything in order."

"For your sake, I hope so, too."

Lydia swallowed the knot in her throat. She didn't want to have to do this again, but from what she understood, if he found anything out of order he'd make her do the whole inspection over. "He's a stickler for the rules," a woman at his office had told her.

"Mind if I look in the kitchen? I've already checked around outside."

"You have?" Lydia placed her hand on her chest. She'd been stewing and praying intermittently for the last two hours, and he'd been out there part of the time.

He nodded. "Already made friends with your pup."

Lydia chuckled nervously. "He's quite a rascal."

"That he is. Smart, though. You ought to think about training him." He pointed toward the kitchen.

"Oh, go ahead. Do I walk around with you or wait or. . ."

"You just hang tight. I'll let you know if I find anything that needs attention."

Lydia sat on the couch. Had George welcomed the man when he walked in the backyard? Actually, Lydia was a little miffed that the dog hadn't barked a stranger warning. But then, George would have to believe he'd met a stranger in order to issue a warning, and George thought he knew everyone.

Sighing, Lydia leaned back on the couch. She grabbed the remote control. Would it be rude to turn on the television while an inspector was in the house? It might seem unprofessional for a future business owner.

She put the controller down and picked up a magazine her mom had accidentally left. Just by skimming the pages, Lydia could tell it was an I-want-the-power magazine. She put it down. She had no need for "the power." God remained her source of power. He proved much better at it than she. Left to herself, Lydia crumbled like a burned piece of toast.

Looking down at her watch, she wondered how long he would take. She knew Lorma was on the edge of her seat, waiting for Lydia to call with the news. Lydia crossed and uncrossed her legs. She twiddled her thumbs and played with her hair. She examined her nails then looked back at her watch. He'd been at it for a good hour. Surely, the man was almost done.

I know, I'll give him a slice of pie for his trouble. She jumped up and headed into the kitchen. *Would that seem like I was trying to bribe him?* She chewed the inside of her lip. When she was in school, the children always teased her about being a teacher's pet because she tried to help out. But really she was just trying to be nice. . .or maybe it was the need to please everyone coming out in her.

She tapped her foot. Opening the cabinet door, she decided being nice was a good Christian quality. She placed two plates on the counter. *If I offer him a piece after he's passed or failed me then I'm not bribing or trying to please. I'm simply being kind.*

She shook her head as she cut two pieces of pie. No one would worry so much about giving someone a dessert. *I've gotta quit overthinking everything.*

"Well, Ms. Hammond, I think I've finished."

Lydia turned around, startled by his abrupt appearance. She searched his face for positive feedback. The man had no expression.

"I need you to sign here." He handed her a paper. She looked at it and tried to see if it said anything about pass or fail. She wasn't sure what it was supposed to say.

"You can open whenever you're ready. You passed."

"Really!" Lydia looked up at him. "Nothing to fix?"

The left side of his mouth lifted slightly upward. The best smile she figured she'd get from the man. "Nothing to fix. You're ready to go."

"Thanks so much." Lydia shook his hand.

The man started to turn toward the door.

"Oh, wait. Would you like a sample of what I'll be serving?"

He raised his eyebrows. "Well, I always have had a weakness for pie."

Lydia pointed toward a chair. "I hope you like it." She watched as the inspector nodded his approval at his first bite of the pie. Excitement filled her heart. She couldn't wait to tell Lorma and Gideon that she'd passed inspection.

Without thinking, she lifted her fingers to her lips, remembering Gideon's touch. Yes, she even wanted to call Gideon.

*

"He's had a heart attack." The doctor rubbed his temple. "He has three blockages. We're going to perform an angioplasty procedure, but I have to warn you, his blockages are quite severe."

Maria gasped, and Gideon held her hand tighter. He knew Mama's arm wrapped around her on the other side.

"Has he had any heart attacks before?" The doctor seemed perplexed, or maybe tired. Gideon wondered how long it had been since the man had slept.

"Not that I know of, but he has been acting different lately."

"How so?"

Maria took a deep breath. "He gets tired easily. Takes a lot of breaks. He's been more irritable."

Yes, Gideon had noticed a change in Jim over the last several weeks, as well. He assumed the older man was worried about Maria. Gideon had been so frustrated with Jim's constant suggestions at matrimony that he hadn't paid attention to the possibility of something else being wrong.

Renewed guilt gnawed at his heart. As the man's employer and as a Christian, he should have been paying better attention. Gideon had been so wrapped up in his own selfishness that he hadn't noticed his own employee—his friend—had grown tired and sick.

"Not all of his tests have come back yet, but considering the degree of blockage, my guess is this is not your father's first heart attack. Has he had any numbness in his arms?"

Worry etched Maria's face. "I guess he has complained a few times, but he'd take an aspirin and sit down awhile." Maria's voice broke, and she tightened her grasp on Gideon's hand. He knew all too well how frightening it was to receive bad news about your father. He looked over at Mama. Unlike Maria, Gideon still had his mother.

"We're getting ready to prep him for surgery. Why don't you come talk to him before he goes? He's awake and stable, just tired."

"Can my friends go, too?"

"Usually we allow only family. . ." The doctor tapped his pen against the clipboard in his hand. His gaze took in Gideon and Mama.

"They are like family to my father. Please." Maria's pleading nearly broke Gideon's heart. She desperately needed comfort.

The doctor tucked his clipboard under his arm. "All right. You'll need to be quick."

Gideon followed Maria, his mother, and the doctor. The last time he'd been in a hospital was when his pa was sick. He hated the smell, hated the pristine cleanness. Everything in him wanted to turn around and walk back outside, but he knew he couldn't. He needed to be there for Jim and Maria.

They turned a corner. He saw Jim. Still pale and listless, but now his eyes were opened slightly.

"Dad?" Maria bent over beside him. Jim tried to lift his hand but could only keep it up a second. The frailty of the man who'd worked so diligently beside him these past two years made Gideon ill. Images of Pa exploded in his mind into so many remembrances that he couldn't sort them out.

Gideon watched as Jim whispered in Maria's ear.

She leaned up and kissed his cheek. "I'll be fine, Dad. I love you. You focus on getting better." She brushed back his hair. "My boys need their grandpa."

A pained expression wrapped Jim's face, and Gideon didn't know if it was physical or emotional. Jim's gaze traveled to Gideon, back to Maria, then to Gideon again. Tightness gripped Gideon's heart. It was Jim's silent message for Gideon to take care of Maria.

Well, I think a person has to evaluate if he understands need from want. Mama's response to Gideon's confusion floated to his mind. She'd spoken the words only moments before Maria burst through the door. Did Gideon understand the difference between need and want? Could he make his heart give up what it desired more than anything? *I must trust You, God, not my heart.*

"Things aren't always what they seem, son."

Gideon flinched as a nurse nudged past him. "All right. It's time to go." The woman lifted the side rails of Jim's bed and walked to the back. She looked at Maria and smiled. "He's in good hands."

Gideon could take no more. He walked out of the room, back down the hall, and out the emergency room doors. Inhaling fresh air as deeply as possible, Gideon closed his eyes. "God, I've made a mistake."

A knot swelled in his throat, and he swallowed hard. "I may have feelings for Lydia, but Maria needs me. There's a difference between need and want, and I can't be selfish. I won't be. Help me, Lord. Help me not love Lydia."

Silence swept through the air. No cars. No sirens. No people. Silence. And God was the quietest of all.

eleven

"Lorma, I passed." Lydia practically squealed as she opened the back door of Gideon's house.

Lorma shouted and jumped, causing her beehive hairdo to wiggle. She wrapped her arms around Lydia. "I'm so proud of you." Lydia enjoyed the older woman's light floral scent mixed with the coffee she'd had that morning.

"And"—Lydia thought her cheeks would bruise if she smiled any fuller as she shifted the plateful of treats from behind her back—"I made the tarts."

"Great-Aunt Mary's tarts!" Lorma's eyes widened and she clapped her hands like a schoolgirl. "I can't wait to taste them."

Lydia giggled. "Okay. You sit down, and I'll get you a cup of milk." Nervousness mixed with her excitement. She wanted Lorma to love these tarts. The woman had been so good to her, and this was the only way Lydia could think of to thank her. She grabbed a cup from the cabinet and opened the refrigerator door. Lydia had spent so much time here that she felt as comfortable in Lorma's kitchen as she did her own.

She poured the milk and set the drink in front of Lorma. Tearing a paper towel off the roll to use as a napkin, she watched as Lorma took a bite. Lorma raised her eyebrows as she chewed. Lydia thought she would die if her friend didn't hurry up and swallow.

Lorma took a drink of milk. "Lydia, they're perfect." Lorma's eyes welled with tears, causing Lydia's to do the same. Lorma stood and hugged Lydia again. "I haven't tasted these in more than forty years."

Lydia squeezed her friend tighter before letting go. "I'm so glad they're right. I wanted to be able to give you something to thank you for..." What could she say? *Thank you for being a friend when I had none. Thank you for being like a mother to me. Thank you for approving of and believing in me. Thank you for welcoming me into the church and community.* Lorma had been and done all those things and more. In Lydia's opinion, God had sent Lorma specifically to be in her life at this time. "I just wanted to thank you for everything."

Lorma patted Lydia's hand. "Lydia Hammond, you are an amazing girl with a wonderful love for people. And what a talent He's given you...to sweeten the lives of others with sweets. Just knowing you is a gift."

"I can't wait to tell Gideon. You know he had to come over and fix my sink the day before inspection." Lydia touched her lips. Just the thought of their sweet kiss spread goose bumps across her skin.

Lorma's expression fell and tears pooled in her eyes. "I'd say he'll be home for lunch, but he probably won't stay long."

Concern pushed the goose bumps aside. When Lorma let out a long sigh and turned toward the refrigerator, Lydia's brain whirled with possibilities. *He couldn't be sick or he would be home. Lorma was all right, or she appeared to be.* Lydia pinched the paper towel between her fingers. "What happened?"

"Jim's had a heart attack."

Sorrow filled Lydia's heart though she had only met Jim one time. She knew he worked the orchards with Gideon and that Maria was his daughter. The man always seemed to scowl at Lydia when she came near, so she stayed away from him. Still, she didn't want him to be sick. "Is he okay?"

"He's in the hospital, recovering from surgery."

"I'm sorry. I'll pray for him."

"Yes. Why don't we do that now?" Lorma grabbed her hands.

"Okay." Lydia's palms began to sweat. She loved talking to God and found herself chatting with Him about every little area of her life, but she still got nervous when it came to praying aloud with others.

Lorma's hands shook just a bit, and Lydia peeked up to see she was crying. "Would you mind praying?" Lorma's voice cracked, and Lydia squeezed her hands tighter.

God, help me. I know I'm just talking out loud to You, but I'm nervous. And I don't know Jim. And I don't think he likes me. She shook her head. *Forgive me, Lord. He's sick, and this isn't about me at all.*

Taking a quick breath, Lydia began. "Dear God, we pray for Jim. He's had a heart attack. . .well, you already know that. But we ask You to be with him. . .of course You're with him. . .but to take care of him. He has family who want to see him better."

God, I'm fumbling this up. I don't know how to pray out loud. I know I'm just talking to You, but just me and You is so different.

She continued, "Take care of Maria and her children, too. Help them. . .be strong. Hold them close. You say we can ask for things, and we ask that Jim get better. Of course, You know what is best, and we do trust You, but we still ask. In the name of Jesus, I pray. Amen."

Lorma squeezed Lydia's hands. "Thank you, dear. Now, let's you and me start some lunch."

&

"Oh no." Gideon saw a brown fur ball that had grown several inches over the last month tied up to his front porch as he drove up the drive. George wagged his tail and barked as Gideon hopped out of the cab and shut the door. The last thing he needed right now was to see Lydia.

Maybe this is Your way of telling me I need to apologize straight up for that kiss since there can't be anything between us. Again, Gideon's prayer seemed to fall flat. It wasn't like he normally heard God's voice booming from the sky, but it had been a long time since Gideon had felt any peace in his relationship with his Savior.

He made his way over to the pup and sat on the porch. George jumped into Gideon's lap. The dog tried to lick every crevice of Gideon's hand. "You're a great protector." Gideon scratched the canine between the ears. "You'd just lick an intruder to death."

For several minutes, Gideon petted Lydia's dog. He looked over the expanse of his property. He wasn't ready to face her. The attraction remained too great, and he knew it was more than just the physical. She oozed spontaneity in her words and actions. She kept him guessing about what she'd say or do next, and he found it refreshing. She'd proved how much she loved people by her treatment of his mom and family, even her little dog. He scratched George's head again.

He even noted her love for God. How many times had he heard her mumbling to herself when he realized she was carrying on complete conversations with God? The simplicity and authenticity of that relationship intrigued him.

She even responded with kindness to Maria when the woman was throwing herself at me in Lydia's own house.

Ugh. He smacked the porch railing. Any man in his right mind would fall in love with Lydia Hammond.

But Gideon couldn't. He had an obligation. A real man cared for the needs of others before his own desires. What was it his teacher had said in school about people of integrity? He snapped his fingers. *They do what's right when no one is looking.* Whether people were looking or not, Gideon loved the Lord, and he would do what was right—care for Maria and her boys.

"Gideon, you're here." Lydia stepped out onto the porch. Her gorgeous hair hung in perfect curls about her shoulders. She must have been wearing some kind of makeup that made the blue in her eyes stand out, because they practically glistened. The pink in her cheeks deepened as she stood looking at him. As always, her beauty shone like a ripened peach.

"Yep." He forced himself to look away from her. At some point, he'd apologize to her. He'd had no right to initiate that kiss. *Though she kissed back, and for a moment I thought all the wrongs in the world had been made right.*

"I'm really sorry about Jim."

The mention of his friend's name brought sense back into Gideon's thick head. He would not think about that kiss again. He was a man, a strong man, and he would control his mind. "Yes, he doesn't appear to be doing well at the moment. He's out of surgery, but he looks awful."

"I'm so sorry."

He heard the door close and thought she'd gone inside until a soft floral scent wafted around him. He felt a light touch on his arm and knew she'd sat beside him. Gritting his teeth, he was determined not to look at her.

"Is there anything I can do?" The concern in her voice sounded sincere, and it nagged at Gideon's heart. Lydia was a sweet, kind woman who deserved a man who would honor, cherish, and protect her. Gideon would have loved to be that man, but it simply wasn't meant to be.

"No."

She touched the top of his hand. Her gentle warmth stirred him. "I do have some good news. It's nowhere near as important as Jim's health, but it might...I don't know."

She removed her hand, and Gideon knew he'd gone from trying to protect himself to being rude. Lydia didn't deserve that. He turned toward her. Again, he couldn't help but notice the adorable freckles sprinkling her nose and the soft curve of her lips. He'd always prided himself on being a man of self-control, but meeting Lydia had proved he wasn't as good at the virtue as he once believed. "Tell me your good news."

Her eyes smiled before her lips had the chance to join them. Her excitement was muted by Jim's illness, but he knew her enough to know it brewed deep within her. "My house passed inspection."

"That's great." Gideon tried to sound happy for her. In truth, he still wasn't convinced the business would succeed, but he wanted to be supportive.

"I was so worried when the faucet started leaking." She ducked her head as her face flamed red. He knew she thought of their kiss. He wondered if it had consumed her mind as much as it had his. Now would be a good time to apologize to her. The sooner, the better. "Lydia, I..."

"There you are." Mama opened the door. "I didn't know what had happened to you, but now I see Gideon's home.

Wonderful! The sandwiches are ready." Mama lifted her finger to the side of her mouth. "You two look absolutely adorable sitting on that porch together."

"Mama"—Gideon frowned and stood to his feet—"we are not teenagers." He noted a pained expression wrapped Lydia's face. She probably felt they would be a couple now. She'd probably even talked to Mama about it.

He was a heel. A big, overgrown heel. How could he have kissed her like that? He knew before he ever went over there that Maria was the woman he should pursue. It was the right thing to do.

God, why does it feel so wrong?

❧

It had been a long time since Lydia had felt so embarrassed. A memory of falling forward down the church steps after a service flashed through her mind. She would have landed flat on her face had the pastor not been there to stop her fall. Even more horrifying was that night at the service the pastor's wife had asked for a prayer for him, as she'd said he'd pinched a nerve in his back earlier that morning. Lydia had taken a pie to the bedridden man, but that didn't lessen her mortification at her clumsiness.

Okay, so embarrassment might as well have been her middle name. Maybe one could look up the word in the dictionary and find Lydia's face pasted to the side, but she still didn't like it. And she especially didn't like that Gideon was being so standoffish just days after he'd kissed her.

She stood and followed Lorma into the house. She'd been convinced the kiss meant something to him. In her mind, it had special significance. It meant they were a couple. Never had she been the kind of girl to kiss a boy on a whim or just because they had gone on a date. Who was she kidding? She'd never really gone on dates, and Gideon's kiss was the first she'd had.

That's why his treatment hurts, Lord.

Straightening her shoulders, she grabbed some bread and meat for her sandwich. She would not show Gideon that his behavior hurt her feelings. Maybe she was being too sensitive. Another trait she'd acquired from somewhere but definitely not from her mother. After all, Jim had just had a heart attack, and Gideon had arrived straight from the hospital less than an hour ago.

That's probably it, God. I'm just being selfish.

She sat at the table and ate a couple of chips. Lorma and Gideon joined her.

Lorma wiped her mouth with her napkin. "We need to do something to celebrate passing inspection."

Lydia covered her mouth and swallowed. "Okay."

"Hmm." Lorma squinted her eyes and tapped the top of her fork against her lips. "I know. Let's go to Royal Theater. A movie made from one of Jane Austen's books is playing this weekend."

Lydia nodded. "That sounds like a lot of fun. I read one of her books in high school."

Lorma looked at her son. "What do you think, Gideon? We could go to the evening show."

"Well, I. . ."

It was obvious Gideon had no desire to go with them. The realization infuriated Lydia. In no way did she want to force him to do anything. "Why don't just you and I go, Lorma?"

"No, no. Don't be silly. Gideon wants to celebrate, too."

The phone rang, and Lorma jumped up. She read the

caller ID and looked at Lydia and Gideon. "It's Chloe. She's probably just gotten back from the obstetrician's office." Lorma's eyes twinkled. "I can't wait for another grandbaby. I'll take it in the other room."

Lorma raced down the hall, leaving Lydia alone with Gideon. If she had been closer to being finished with her lunch, she'd have left, but with most of her sandwich still uneaten, she didn't want to be wasteful. She focused on her plate, determined not to talk to the man who wanted nothing to do with her.

"Lydia, we need to talk." Gideon's voice sounded low and had a pained edge to it.

"Sure." She traced a chip around her plate but didn't look up at him.

"It's about the kiss the other night."

Lydia shrugged her shoulders, trying to act nonchalant. She knew this wasn't going to be a now-we're-a-couple speech. His actions expressed nothing more than a desire to get as far away from her as he could. Her appetite fled. No way could she finish the rest of her sandwich. She inwardly contemplated how she was going to finish the rest of this conversation without crying. "What about it?"

"I shouldn't have. . ."

She lifted her hand to silence him. Hurt, pure and powerful, welled inside her. She didn't want to hear anything else he had to say. "Look, we can forget about it."

"But I'm sorry."

Anger laced through her pain. "I said just forget about it. It didn't—" She knew the words about to spill from her mouth were a lie. A stronger person would have just told the truth and accepted the rejection head on. She wasn't a stronger person. "It didn't mean anything."

"I see."

Lydia sneaked at peek at him, noting the pain that wrapped his face. Why would he look stricken? He was the one rejecting her. She didn't want to think about it. She just wanted to leave, to get as far away from him as she could. "I've got to go. . .feed George." Another lie. The dog ate when he wanted. "Tell Lorma I said bye."

She picked up her plate and stood. The chair fell backward behind her and smashed to the floor. "Oh." Without looking up, Lydia turned and picked it up.

Her nerves started to get the best of her, and her hands started to shake. *Just make it to the trash and leave. It's not that hard. Please, Lord, it's not that hard.*

After throwing away what she couldn't give George, she placed her plate in the sink. Still avoiding eye contact, she ducked her head and made a beeline out the door.

"Come on, George." She reached for George's leash, slipped, and stepped on his paw. He yelped, and the emotion Lydia had bottled filled her eyes. "I'm sorry, buddy."

"Are you okay?" Gideon's voice sounded behind her, just inside the door.

She would not let him see her cry. Not again. She'd never allow herself to be vulnerable in front of him again. "We're fine."

She unhooked George and jumped off the porch in one motion. Gideon Andrews and his kiss meant nothing to her. She stomped toward the well-worn path that led to her house.

Maybe if I keep saying that to myself, it will come true.

twelve

Lydia grabbed a wad of paper towels off the roll. She scrunched them in her hand then smashed the black ants that had made a trail up her cabinet and across the counter. "Ugh. I hate bugs." She'd sprayed around the house twice, but she couldn't seem to get rid of the pests.

Glancing in her sink, she sighed. *It might have something to do with the fact that I haven't washed dishes in days.* Stacks of grimy dishes and even a moldy cup of milk stared up at her. She just hadn't been in the mood to do anything.

Forcing herself to turn on the faucet, she grabbed the bottle of dish soap and poured a generous amount into the streaming water. *If I let them soak a few minutes before I put them in the dishwasher, the gunk will come off easier.*

Once the sink filled, she turned the faucet off and padded in her oversized kitty slippers into the living area. A myriad of wrappers and open soft drink cans, a pizza box, and a half-eaten, melted tub of ice cream greeted her. *I'm going to have to put cockroach traps out if I don't get a handle on this.*

She wrapped her robe tighter around her waist. After grabbing a handful of trash, she wrinkled her nose when her finger slipped into the goopy ice-cream container. *This is ridiculous. I've been pouting like a jilted teenager. And it's about time I stop.* She sucked in a long breath and crammed the stuff into the garbage can. But she felt like a jilted teenager.

Gideon's kiss was her first ever. She knew she was a bit old to have never been kissed, but she'd always been so silly and clumsy. In school she was everyone's friend, but no one's date. Which suited her just fine. She never knew when she might step on a guy's foot dancing, claw him if they held hands, or something worse.

The intense feelings she bore for Gideon were foreign to her. She didn't know how to handle them. And she certainly hadn't expected a simple kiss to pain her so deeply.

I'm just going to take a little nap, and then I'll clean this house. She made her way into her bedroom and took in the disheveled bed covers, the dirty clothes lying on the floor, and the additional mess of leftover junk food. After slipping into her bed, George jumped up beside her. The pup wagged his tail then rested his chin on the bed covers.

Feeling sorry for the little guy, she scratched his head. "You've been my faithful little friend, haven't you?"

George sat up on the bed and barked. He nestled his way closer to her, trying to get her to play. She petted his head and forced a smile to spread her lips. "After a nap, okay?"

Seeming to understand what she said, George circled a spot on the bed several times, trying to make himself comfortable. He finally settled in, and Lydia lay back on her pillow and closed her eyes. No matter how many different images she tried to conjure, her mind always returned to Gideon.

"Please, God, take him out of my thoughts." She grabbed a pillow and covered her head with it.

The doorbell rang, and George leaped from the bed, barking wildly. Lydia didn't move. *Maybe they'll think I'm not home and leave.* A few seconds passed, and the doorbell rang again. George's barks echoed through the otherwise silent house.

"Please go away," Lydia mumbled into the pillow. The only people she could think would visit her would be Lorma or Gideon, and she wasn't up to seeing either one of them.

A chorus of knocks sounded from the door. George's wild barks filled the air. The poor pup was going to collapse if he didn't find out who was behind that door. Frustrated, Lydia pulled herself out of bed. She glanced into a mirror and rolled her eyes. Raking her fingers through her nappy hair, she scowled. *I can always say I'm desperately sick.*

Another lie. It seemed the fibs stepped one on top of the other ever since the kiss. *This is why being single is much better.* Now, if she could just convince her heart of that.

The adamant visitor knocked several times more. "I'm coming," Lydia yelled. *If I open the door and it's a solicitor, I'm liable to give them a piece of my mind.*

Finally making her way to the front door, she opened it. Her mother, dressed in a bright red summer dress, stood with her back to Lydia. Her hand swept the expanse of the front yard as she mumbled, "That girl's not even keeping Mother's place properly mowed. What was I thinking. . ."

Lydia swallowed hard. The yard appeared in desperate need of mowing, and she hadn't weeded the flower gardens in over a week. The house looked far worse than the yard. Embarrassment flooded her. She had no business letting Grandma's house go as she had. It wasn't the property's fault Lydia's heart had been stomped on by its neighbor. "Hello, Mom."

The older woman turned gracefully around. Large, dark sunglasses covered a flawless makeup-painted face. Her mother's lips set in a deep frown. "Are you sick, Lydia?"

Lydia bit her bottom lip. She tightened the knot in her

robe. "I guess I haven't felt well."

Rita took her sunglasses off her face and peered past the door. Lydia gripped the robe belt tighter as she imagined what her mother thought of the obvious mess behind her daughter. For the first time, Lydia noted the red and blue pin below her mother's shoulder that read "Vote for Hammond." Two yard signs dangled from her mother's grasp. "Are you going to let me in?"

Lydia nodded and opened the door wide. She stood silent when her mother walked in and gasped. Scanning the room, Lydia realized it was even worse than she'd first noticed. Books, magazines, blankets, shoes, clothes, wrappers, and other unidentifiable things dotted the room. She closed her eyes, praying the kitchen wasn't sporting additional ants.

The scowl deepened on her mother's face when she turned to Lydia. "Do you feel well enough to help me clean this up?"

"Yes."

"Well enough to get out of your pajamas?"

"Yes."

Her mother opened her arms wide as if showcasing the room. "May we get started?"

Nodding, Lydia made her way to her bedroom to change clothes. She could have been bedridden with the flu and double pneumonia, and her mother would still have been furious. With everything in her, Lydia wished she could share her heartache with her mother, but she knew that wasn't possible.

Rita Louise Hammond was a goal-oriented, strong woman. Things ran smoothly in her life. There was no time for emotional tirades or fits of self-pity. Her mother would have never allowed her heart to become so consumed by a man in the first place.

Lydia was so different from her mother. At this moment, a bit of her mom's coarse temperament would have been nice. It might take away some of the sting of Gideon's rejection.

No. Deep in the core of her heart, Lydia knew she didn't want to be like her mother. God wanted her to have a tender heart, and tender hearts would inevitably experience times of pain.

But, God, I've tried to be a witness to Mom. She's such a strong woman. She needs to see strong women who adore You. All she sees from me is weakness. Lydia shook her head. God was the master of taking weakness and making it strong. He could take this time of hurt and make her stronger, as well.

Inhaling the hope that God remained in control, Lydia quickly made her bed and gathered the dirty clothes off the floor. After throwing them in the hamper, she collected the trash off the end table and threw it away.

With her chin up, she walked into the kitchen. Disgust wrapped her mother's features as she scrubbed the dishes in the sink. Lydia noted a black ant scurrying down the side of the cabinet. She grabbed another paper towel, swiped him up, and threw him away. "I'll get it, Mom."

"How many days have you been sick?" Her mother's eyes lit with anger instead of compassion.

"I haven't been myself for just a few days." Lydia longed to be able to confide in her mother the true reason for her sickness, but she could tell it would only infuriate her more. "Here, let me do that. Go get your things. How long are you staying?"

Her mother handed Lydia the dishrag. "I planned to stay one night, but if you're this sick"—she swiped her hand around the destroyed kitchen—"then I'm not sure I want to risk getting what you have."

Lydia blew a strand of hair away from her eyes. She'd have no choice but to fess up. "I'm not *that* sick. I've been upset."

"You let Mother's house go like this because you've been upset?" Rita rested her hands on her hips. "Honestly, Lydia. Maybe Grace is right about you needing to make your own way."

"What?" Lydia lifted her shoulders. "Aunt Grace wants me to leave?"

Rita shook her head. "No. No. That's taken care of." She pointed at Lydia. "I'm going to town to see about putting a few signs in front of businesses. When I get back, I want this place cleaned up."

"Okay, Mom." Lydia watched as her mother stomped out the front door. Within moments, Lydia heard tires spitting gravel from the driveway. Her mother hadn't even bothered to ask about Lydia's concerns. As always, her own mother really didn't care.

⁂

Gideon moved the love seat to the only empty place in the living area. "How's this, Mama?" He watched as she scratched the side of her head, making the whole wrapping of salt-and-pepper hair move. How many years had Mama worn her hair in that knot on the top of her head? Too many to count.

"I'm just not sure. Maybe if we move the couch over here and the love seat over there." She pointed to the other side of the room. "Maybe it would balance more."

"Mama, I just moved them out of those spots." Gideon kneaded the middle of his back with his hand. "All this moving is killing me."

"Hogwash." Mama swatted the air with her hand. "You're young and fit as a fiddle."

"Hmm." Gideon wiped his brow with the back of his hand. "Maybe if you feed me a bit of that strawberry cheesecake in the kitchen, it will recharge my battery, and I'll be able to move all this stuff again."

"You think so?" Mama crossed her arms in front of her chest and smiled.

"Yep."

"All right then." She patted his shoulder then headed into the kitchen. "A break it is."

Gideon poured cups of coffee for both of them while Mama cut good-sized slices of the dessert. They sat at the table, and Gideon cut a piece of the cheesecake and slipped it into his mouth. "Mmm. This is good."

"I can't make apple tarts as good as Lydia, but I do make a mean strawberry cheesecake."

Gideon's heart sank at the mention of Lydia. He'd been unable to keep her from his thoughts. His heart still hurt from her admission that their kiss didn't mean anything to her. He'd kissed less than a handful of girls in his life, and hers had meant more to him than he had expected.

"Speaking of Lydia"—Mama wiped her mouth with a napkin—"have you heard from her lately?"

"Not since she was here last." Gideon glanced down at his watch. *Seven days and a little over two hours ago.* He huffed at the realization that he had actually counted the hours since he'd seen her last. A man who intended to take care of another woman as a life commitment should not think in such ways.

"I haven't heard from her either." Mama scrunched her face in concern. "That's odd. She usually calls several times a week, at least every two or three days."

"Does she?" Of course he knew she called so often. Just hearing Mama's light chuckles when she talked on the phone with Lydia made Gideon feel closer to her. He knew she hadn't called. It had taken every ounce of strength he had not to race over to her house to make sure she was okay. A good neighbor would do it just out of concern, but Gideon knew his heart. He would do it because of his love. A love that he had to squelch.

Lord, help me overcome these feelings for Lydia—

"Have you heard from Maria?" Mama's question interrupted Gideon's plea.

"No. The last time I talked to her, Jim was resting fine at home. Weak but stable."

"I'm going to make some soup to take over to them later. You can go with me." Mama got up and put her plate in the sink.

Yes, visiting Maria and Jim would be good. The more time Gideon spent with Maria, the more God would allow his feelings for her to grow.

"Let's finish moving the furniture."

Gideon smiled at the commanding tone in Mama's voice. The fact that she'd kept him busy was a blessing, as well. A tired body didn't have much time to think about silly things like curly, reddish-blond hair, light blue eyes, and sprinklings of freckles.

He growled. *There's not enough work in the world to keep my mind off that woman.*

⠎

Lydia pulled the tarts from the oven. Her mom had been gone for a little over two hours. Though she hadn't had time to mow the lawn, Lydia was able to get the house cleaned, weed the flower gardens, and whip up some apple tarts. Most importantly, she'd been able to spend some time in God's Word and in prayer. Something she hadn't done much of the last several days. Wallowing in pity had a way of taking one's focus off the blessings God had given. Lydia was thankful her mom had given her the opportunity to reevaluate.

The sweet, fruity scent filled the air, and Lydia breathed it in. "Mmm. I hope Mom likes these as much as Lorma."

As if on cue, Lydia heard the slamming of a car door outside. She made her way to the front door and opened it before her mom had crossed the sidewalk.

"Hi, Mom."

"Well, don't you look different." Her mother's smile was one Lydia recognized all too well. It was the simpering, eat-you-up one that she used on clients and now potential voters. In truth, Lydia believed her mother to be a good candidate for office. She wasn't a Christian, but she had high morals, good ethics, and an intelligent, analytical mind. Lydia also knew her mom had a disconnect when it came to feeling, and she sometimes wondered if her mom even had emotions.

"Were you able to put up all your signs?"

"Yes, I was." Her mother pulled her sunglasses off her face as she walked onto the porch.

"I made some tarts for you." Lydia stepped back when her mother walked through the door. A wave of perfume fought the fruity smell for dominance.

"Great. I'm famished. It'll be just the snack I need before I change and we go out for dinner." She peered at Lydia. "You'll need to put on something a bit nicer, as well."

Lydia looked down at her capris and blouse. This was one of her favorite outfits. In her opinion, it was totally appropriate for any restaurant in Danville. It pained her that she never felt good enough for her mom. Never. Closing her eyes, she remembered the scriptures she'd read about pleasing God over men. *I won't let Mom's insensitivity hurt me. I have a couple dresses she approves of. I'll just change for her and go to dinner. No big deal.*

She followed her mom into the kitchen, wishing her heart believed what her mind told her. *God, You'll have to keep helping me not to be hurt because I'm not good enough for her.*

A wave of self-pity washed over her being. *I wasn't good enough for Gideon, either.* Fighting back the tears that threatened to flood her face, Lydia glanced at the ceiling, allowing her inner groans of unworthiness to beseech her God's assistance. Her head knew her worth came from God; she'd have to trust her heart to Him as well. A moment of authentic forgiveness for Gideon and her mother filled her. Lydia watched as her mother grabbed a plate and napkin. She scooped an apple tart off the cooling rack and bit into it. Rita's eyes widened in surprise. "This is wonderful."

Lydia's heart swelled, not only at her mom's praise but at the awareness that God would always give her what she needed from Him. "Thanks."

Her mother shook her head. "No, I mean this may be the best tart I've ever tasted."

Lydia bit her lip, willing her eyes not to tear up. Finally, her mom showed a moment of approval.

Rita popped the last of the tart into her mouth. She wiped her hands on the napkin. "You should do quite well with the coffee shop."

Lydia felt she could soar through the air. Pleasure filled her body and straightened her shoulders. "Thanks, Mom."

Rita threw the napkin in the trash. She opened the dishwasher and stuck the plate inside. Looking up at Lydia, she grimaced. "That is if you can handle the business aspect of it." With a sigh and a fling of her wrist, she walked out of the room. "I suppose we'll find out soon enough."

Lydia's joy plummeted for a brief moment. *Oh, Jesus, this is why my focus must always be on You. Your pleasure and approval alone are all I should strive for.* A vision of Gideon's rejection filled her mind and mingled with her mother's dismissal. *God, You may be the only one who will approve of me anyway.*

thirteen

"Mama, what do you mean you can't go to the movie?" Gideon gripped the back of the chair so hard he thought the wood might split in two. "This was your idea."

"I know. I know." Mama nodded her head as she shoved a casserole dish of some kind into the oven. "But Maria's babysitter is sick, Jim isn't feeling well either, and Maria has to work."

Gideon released the chair and kneaded the back of his neck. He'd had double the load of work on the orchard with Jim being sidelined. He wanted Jim to take all the time he needed to get better, and Gideon wouldn't consider not paying Jim while he was down. Jim had been too faithful of an employee for too many years. However, because he still paid Jim, that left him no extra income with which to hire additional help. He didn't begrudge a penny of it, but Gideon sure felt tired. This trip to the Royal Theater had actually been an excursion he'd looked forward to for most of the week. Of course, he wasn't thrilled they'd be watching a chick flick of some kind and he'd have to deal with his conflicted feelings while sitting near Lydia.

"Mama, you have to go." He smacked his hand against the counter. "We'll take the boys with us."

"To see *Sense and Sensibility*?" She chuckled. "They'd last about two minutes."

"Well, I don't want to see some silly girl movie either. You

122

go, and I'll watch the boys."

"No. You need a break."

"Mama."

"And it's a wonderful, silly girl movie." She laughed out loud. "My overgrown son needs to get in touch with his soft side. He's been overly bristly of late."

"Mama."

"Don't 'Mama' me." She pointed her finger at him. "You're going. You will rest. You will be nice." Though he knew she tried to sound firm, a smile lifted her lips. "And you will have fun."

"Fine, Mama." Gideon grabbed his keys off the rack and walked out the door. Arguing with his mother always proved useless. It had for Pa, and it did for Gideon, as well.

"I told her we'd take her to dinner, too," she yelled from the kitchen. "Be sure you feed her."

"Sure, Mama, whatever you say." *Should I take her shopping for a new dress, maybe take her to get a haircut, too?* He knew if Mama wanted it, he'd end up doing what she asked. Trying to ignore the spark of excitement at having the chance to spend time with Lydia alone, Gideon hopped into his truck. If he allowed honesty to take precedence, he would admit taking Lydia anywhere would be complete pleasure.

He blew out a long breath. He couldn't allow those feelings. The last thing he needed was to spend time alone with Lydia. Every time he thought of her, which was too many times to count, he saw the pained expression on her face when they spoke of the kiss. Her it-didn't-mean-anything answer still pricked his heart, but he couldn't seem to stop caring for her.

But I can control my actions. Maria and I have gotten along well for some time now. I enjoy being around her and the boys.

With Jim being so sick, they needed him now. He peered at his reflection in the rearview mirror. "And you'd do good to remember that."

&

Lydia fell back onto the couch and flopped her feet on the coffee table while she waited for Lorma and Gideon to pick her up. Overall, she'd had a good visit with her mom. Rita hadn't liked the dress Lydia picked for dinner, but she'd bragged to the waiter about Lydia opening a coffee shop. Rita hadn't like the paint color or the furniture Lydia had bought for the shop, but she'd commented that maybe once the customers tried the desserts they'd be fine. Rita had also been critical about the drive the customers would have to make, the lack of signs, the yard that needed attention, and so many other things that Lydia couldn't keep them all straight in her mind.

Gideon, too, had expressed concern about the drive. Lydia and Lorma had only talked about that aspect of the business a few times. Lorma remained convinced that once customers tried the shop, they'd keep coming and bring friends, but after listening to her mother, Lydia was a bit concerned. The fact remained that no one would just happen to drive by her coffee shop without reason. She lived only a few miles away from town, not too far by any means, but still far enough that no one would just "happen by."

Queasiness filled her stomach. What if Gideon was right? He hadn't said much lately, but she knew he felt the shop was a foolhardy idea. He hadn't wanted her to borrow money for something that would flop, which really infuriated her. He'd made several assumptions without realizing she wasn't borrowing any money to start her business. *I am using the largest chunk of my savings and inheritance though.*

She swept the thought away. She was just getting nervous because she was so close to being ready to open the coffee shop. Thinking about Gideon only brought a mixture of fury and pain anyway. Rejection and condemnation seemed to accompany Gideon when she saw him. Quite frankly, she'd had enough of both in her life with her mother. She would not tolerate any from some overgrown grouch of a man.

A vision of Gideon being attacked by his nieces came to her mind. She remembered him helping his mother in the kitchen. She thought of how much George loved him and how many people in their community seemed to have a great deal of respect for Gideon.

Okay, okay. So Gideon's not an ogre. It's just me he has a problem with.

She huffed. George's ears perked up, and he jumped on the couch beside her. She petted her fast-growing pup. "What have I ever done to rile his feathers?" George turned his head, trying to lick her hand. She grinned. "Besides saying things I shouldn't, allowing you to ruin his peaches, knocking over a chair, and a number of other catastrophes."

She laughed out loud. "God, it's a good thing I'm trying to please You and not men."

Gravel popped in her driveway, alerting her that Lorma and Gideon had arrived. She stood and grabbed her purse off the coffee table. "I'll see you later." She bent down and petted George's head one last time. After making her way out the door, she locked it and turned toward the sidewalk. Her heart sped up when she looked at her ride.

Gideon sat in the truck—alone.

❧

Gideon crunched a handful of popcorn. He thought of the surprised look on Lydia's face when she first walked out her door. The drop in her expression said it all when he'd told her that Mama couldn't go with them to the movie. He shoved another handful of popcorn into his mouth. *Well, I didn't want to come alone either. Mama and her bright ideas.* "We'll take Lydia to a movie and dinner to celebrate," Mama's words echoed through his mind. The "we'll" had changed too quickly in Gideon's opinion.

Maybe it was her sweet perfume that kept distracting him, or the fact that she'd swept the sides of her hair up into some kind of clip at the back of her head. Seeing the line of her jaw and the length of her neck, he'd immediately remembered the softness of her skin. He shifted in his chair. He did not need to think about such things. *If this movie would just start, I could concentrate on it and not on her.*

As if on cue, the lights dimmed and the screen sprang to life. Attempting to focus on the commercials, he tried to ignore the light crunch of popcorn as she took small bites. *Even her snacking is distracting me.*

He had to get out of there. If only for a moment. He leaned over. He must have surprised her because she jerked and faced him. Their eyes met. She sucked in her breath and pursed her lips. His lips were mere inches from hers. Immediate need to claim them again surged through him. He broke eye contact. "I'll be right back."

Racing to the back of the theater, Gideon made his way to the restroom. Once there, he turned on the faucet and splashed cool water on his face. This was torture. Complete and utter torture. He loved this woman for her sweetness, her tenderness, her genuine care for others. He loved her spontaneity and the fact that she carried no secrets. And yes, he had to admit his attraction for her. She had captivated him the moment he'd met her.

But the way he felt when he was with her completely took him by surprise. He wanted to protect her from anything that would ever hurt her. He wanted to wrap his arms around her and claim her as his one and only. He longed to love her openly and without reservation. With Lydia, he'd feel what he watched his parents share.

But it's not to be. God, help me. My Christian duty is to care for those who need care. Lydia doesn't need me.

She doesn't?

Gideon closed his eyes to the question that formed in his mind. Lydia was a strong, capable woman full of life and energy. She loved the Lord and sought His guidance. Maria was the one who needed his help. She needed him to take care of her.

Are you the great Provider?

The thought that pricked Gideon's heart humbled him. Was he taking matters into his own hands? Was Gideon not showing God the faith He required and deserved?

Gideon dried his hands and face with a paper towel. He stared at his reflection in the mirror. Dark bags hung under his eyes, proof that sleep had evaded him several nights in a row and that he'd put in extra hours of labor in the orchard. Weariness, in body and spirit, had become his best friend.

God alone knew what Lydia and Maria needed, but Gideon also knew God placed people in his and others' lives to help them along the way. Maria needed someone to care for her. No one denied that. It was obvious to Jim, to

Maria, and Gideon. These questions pounding his mind were simply Gideon's own selfish desires to find a way to pursue a relationship with Lydia. And Gideon refused to be selfish.

❧

"I should be ready to open for business in a month." Lydia cut off a piece of her sirloin and dipped it in steak sauce. She'd started every possible conversation she could think of with Gideon. Anything to keep her from thinking about his amazing eyes or the perfect tone of his tanned skin.

"That's great."

She watched as Gideon stabbed his fork into his baked potato. The man must have had a vendetta against the vegetable. *Or maybe it's me.* She shoved the piece of meat into her mouth. It wasn't her fault that Lorma hadn't been able to go to the movie with them. No one forced Gideon to take her. *Well, that's probably not true. I'm sure Lorma didn't give him any other options.*

Lydia pierced her fork through the green beans. Still, she had tried to keep a positive outlook. She'd enjoyed the movie. *Sense and Sensibility* was one of her favorites. But she'd also been aware that Gideon felt less than comfortable. The fact that he'd gone to the restroom at least three times proved it.

She sneaked a peek at the man across the table from her. A frown etched his jaw while his gaze stayed focused on his plate. Fury erupted within her. She'd given him no reason to behave in such an unfriendly manner. "Gideon, is something wrong?" She knew the words snapped from her mouth, but she'd had it with him.

"Nope." He didn't look up, just jabbed his meat.

"Are you sure?"

"Yep."

Lydia chewed on the inside of her lip, watching as Gideon shoved part of his roll into his mouth. He still hadn't looked up at her. "I'm thinking I must have offended you in some way. I know we didn't part on the best of terms. . ." The memory of his rejection swelled within her heart and threatened to spill from her lips. She fought it back. "But I thought we were going to try to be. . .friends."

Oh, how she didn't want to be friends. Being Gideon's friend was like denying her heart the right to beat. Even as he sat across from her, unwilling to make eye contact, she still longed for a relationship with him—one that entailed love and commitment.

Gideon blew out a long breath and leaned back in his seat. He looked up at her for the first time. "You're right. I'm just very preoccupied." He twisted the fork. "I'm sorry."

True repentance wrapped his features. Forgiveness replaced her anger. She knew he'd had a hard few weeks. "I know you've been busy. If it was too much for you to get away this evening, I would have understood."

He shook his head. "No, I needed some time away."

She'd spent several days wrapped up in self-pity over this man's rejection. But now, she felt an overwhelming compassion for him. Her attraction to him still existed. She couldn't deny that. If she were completely honest, she knew she cared for him as she'd never cared for another man. But at this moment, she knew he needed friendship, and she could offer that. She reached across the table and touched the top of his hand.

He jerked but didn't move away.

"I'll be praying for you."

"Thanks." His features seemed to carry a burden greater

than he confessed as he pulled his hand away from hers.

She noted a longing in his eyes that she couldn't quite decipher, but she didn't try to either.

An overwhelming peace invaded Lydia's soul. From the depths of her heart, she wanted Gideon's best. His best didn't have to include her, and unbelievably, she felt at peace about that. God's will was the most important thing in both their lives, and if friendship was what God designed for them, then who was she to argue with her heavenly Father.

Tears filled her eyes and she wiped them away. *God, I truly am learning that Your pleasure is more important than mine. Thank You, Jesus.*

fourteen

Gideon dropped Lydia off at her house and drove home. The evening had been a complete wreck. All he could think about was how much he cared for Lydia. In the midst of being consumed with his feelings, he'd been a jerk all evening.

After pulling the key from the ignition, he slipped outside and gently closed the door. He needed some time alone. Just him and God. He needed to get down to the nitty-gritty of his battle between love for Lydia and duty to Maria. He'd had all a man could take.

He took determined steps toward the orchard. With fall quickly approaching, his trees had grown to their peaks. The apples blossomed more scrumptious looking every day. Shoving his hands deep into his pockets, he peered up at the heavens that shone between the trees. "God, I can't do this anymore. I'm not hearing from You, and I can't turn off the feelings I have for Lydia."

The wind whispered back to him as it drifted past branches and leaves. He noted the dotting of stars in the vast expanse above him. If God could create the heavens and the earth, He could tell Gideon what to do about Lydia and Maria.

"Maria needs me, God. She has no husband and two boys to care for. But I love Lydia. To the depth of my core, I know I love her. I love her smile, her sweet expressions. I love her clumsiness and spontaneity. I love her love for people." He lifted his hands to his chest, never taking his gaze off the heavens above him. "But isn't it selfish for me to want Lydia when it is Maria who has the need?"

Please God, not men. The gist of the Galatians verse he'd heard on Mama's CD filled his heart. But what pleased God? Both women were Christians. This wasn't a matter of following scripture; it was a matter of the heart. If there were no circumstances involved, he wouldn't even consider Maria as a mate.

The admission tore at him. Would it be fair to spend his life with a woman whom he would have never considered if it weren't for her circumstances?

Shaking his head, he knelt in the middle of the path. "God, I need Your will. Whatever it is, show me."

His phone vibrated in his pocket. He pulled it out and pushed TALK. "Hello."

"Gideon, it's Maria. I need you to come to the hospital right now."

☙

"Mom, where are we going?" Lydia had to raise her voice over the mufflers, whistles, and horns—a typical Indianapolis symphony. She tried to keep up with her mother's quick pace across the street. The woman walked at record speed despite the fact that she had on three-inch heels.

"My office. We have some business to settle."

Apprehension welled in Lydia's gut. She had no more than walked into the house after going to the movies and dinner with Gideon when her mother called and said she'd be at Lydia's first thing in the morning. She wouldn't tell Lydia what happened, just that Lydia had no choice but to join her for legal matters.

Lydia scaled the steps outside the high-rise building her

mother worked at in the city. The air felt thick and heavy and seemed to weigh down on Lydia. The chatter of people and ringing cell phones, and a myriad of other sounds, caused her head to pound. They walked into some semblance of quiet and order once inside the building, but Lydia could barely keep up with her mom's staccato steps across the polished floors and into the nearest elevator.

Silence wrapped the crowded area when several people joined them on their quest for a floor above the first. The lighted number four and accompanying *beep* notified them they had reached her mother's floor. Before the doors had opened fully, her mom grabbed her hand and led her out. Lydia breathed a sigh of relief and took a moment to catch her breath when she finally read her mother's name, along with several others, on a plate beside an ornate door.

"Come on." Her mom grabbed her hand again and led her through the office. She didn't stop to say hello to anyone.

Lydia tried to nod and smile, but their breakneck speed did little to invite proper greetings.

Rita abruptly stopped outside a solid black door, but Lydia wasn't prepared and ran smack into the back of her mother. Rita pushed her off. "Really, Lydia." She smoothed the front of her skirt. "Straighten yourself up."

"What's going on, Mom?"

A determined expression crossed Rita's face as she grabbed the doorknob. "You'll find out soon enough." She opened the door, and Lydia peered inside.

"Hello, Lydia."

Panic wrapped around Lydia's chest when the older woman, dressed in a long black dress, stood to her feet. Lydia swallowed the golf-ball-sized knot that had instantaneously formed in her throat. "Hello, Aunt Grace."

&

Gideon watched as his mother wrapped Maria in an embrace. Sobs poured from the younger woman, and Gideon could do nothing but watch as her back heaved with the immense emotion. Mama crooned at her, patting her back and hair. Gideon's body seemed to have rooted itself to the floor. He shifted his gaze to the hospital bed. The sheets were rumpled. Only minutes ago it had held his friend and employee.

But now it was empty, and Jim was dead.

This scene proved too familiar to him. It brought back too many memories of his pa's death. His sisters crying. His mother crying. Pats on the back. Too many hugs. He hated the smell of a hospital.

Gideon scanned the room. "Where are the boys?" Concern for the two guys filled his heart. They loved their grandpa so much.

"Oh." Maria released herself from Mama and wiped her eyes. "They're with a nurse out front." She wiped her nose on a tissue. "I've got to get hold of myself and go see them. They'll be terrified if they see me like this."

"I'll go." The words slipped through Gideon's mouth before he'd had a chance to think. The boys would have questions that he didn't want to answer, wasn't sure it was his place to answer. "What should I tell them. . .if they ask?"

"You don't need to do that, Gideon." She sucked in a deep breath. "I'm okay. I'll go get the boys."

Mama touched her arm. "You're not okay, dear. Let Gideon see to the boys for a moment."

Maria's bottom lip quivered as she nodded. "You don't have to tell them anything. If they ask. . ." She flailed her arm through the air. "I don't know. Bring them to me."

Gideon forced his feet to lift off the floor and moved toward the entrance of the hospital. Just as Maria had said, the boys sat in an office with a young woman. She looked up at Gideon as he approached. An expression of pity covered her features. "Hey guys, what are you doing?" Gideon kneeled to the boys' level.

Jeremy shoved a piece of scribbled paper in his face. "Color."

"That's great, Jer." Gideon tousled his hair and turned toward Kelbe. The young boy's face drew into a deep frown.

"Where's grandpa?"

"Well. . ."

"Is he still sick?" Kelbe laid his paper on the chair. "I want to go see him."

"Well, Kelbe. . ."

Before Gideon could answer, Maria swept into the room. Tears still filled her eyes as she bent down and scooped her boys into an embrace. "I couldn't let you tell the boys. I have to do it."

Gideon nodded and stood to his feet. He watched as Maria explained that Grandpa wouldn't be going home with them, that he'd gone home to Jesus. The boys' incessant questions and Maria's patient dealing with their loss tore at his heart. He felt like an intruder and yet knew he needed to be there.

God, I guess this is my answer.

❧

Lydia's mom motioned for her to have a seat beside her aunt. Lydia feared they could hear her knees knocking together as she tried to obey her mother's gesture. She had a feeling she knew what this was about. Dread stirred inside her.

Taking her seat, she turned to her aunt. "Do you need me for something?"

"I want my share of the house."

Lydia's heart raced at the words she'd heard. She didn't have any money to give her aunt. She'd have to move. After all the work and planning, after all the sweat and excitement, she'd have to pack her things and move. But where? *God, what am I to do?*

"Now, wait a minute, Grace." Her mother's voice penetrated Lydia's thoughts. Rita leaned forward in the plush leather chair behind the desk. Lydia hadn't even realized her mother had walked away from the door, let alone taken a seat. "Surely we can work something out."

Aunt Grace nodded her head, causing the perfect dark brown curls around her face to bounce. "Yes, we can sell the house, and I will collect my portion of the money."

Lydia gasped.

"But Grace"—her mother curled her fingers together and laid them on top of the desk—"Lydia has put a lot of work into the house. A lot of her own money. I told you she was opening a coffee shop."

"I never said she could open a shop." Her aunt's stare bore into Lydia. "And no one asked me either."

"I'm sorry." Lydia wrapped her fingers around the strap on her purse. "I just assumed..."

"Never assume, young lady. You could have had the common courtesy to ask my opinion before you decided to try to make money off my mother's property."

Guilt filled Lydia's heart. She hadn't asked Aunt Grace's opinion. She'd talked to her mother, but Aunt Grace owned half the house. It was her right to know what Lydia decided to do with the home. Obviously, the oversight had meant a lot to her aunt. She turned to face her aunt more fully. "You're right. I'm sorry. I didn't think. . ."

"That's right, you didn't think. You never think. You just go and do and never think about what it will cost others."

Lydia sucked in her breath.

"That's enough, Grace." Lydia looked at her mother. The protective tone in her voice was one that Lydia had never known. Rita stood to her feet and walked around the desk. She leaned against it and clasped her hands. "What if I buy your half from you?"

"What?" Lydia and Aunt Grace said at the same time.

"I'll buy your half. I think Lydia has a good thing going on over there. I think her business will do well." She shrugged her shoulders. "And if it doesn't, it won't be because she hasn't put a lot of planning into it."

Lydia couldn't speak. Her mother had obviously stunned her aunt as well, because Grace didn't say anything for several minutes.

"If it's the money you want, you have no choice legally but to be willing to let me purchase your half."

"I know." The fury behind Aunt Grace's words was palpable, and Lydia shivered.

"Then I guess it's settled." Her mom slipped behind the desk again. "I'll have the papers written up."

Lydia watched in stunned silence as her aunt and mother discussed various legalities. Her mother believed in what she was doing. For the first time in her life, Rita Louise Hammond thought Lydia was doing something worthwhile. The magnitude of it rocked Lydia's core, and she didn't know what to think, what to feel, what to say.

After some time, Grace stood and peered down at Lydia. "Don't mess this up for your mother."

Her words were harsh, and they hurt, but the fact that her mother had faith in her overshadowed anything her aunt could do or say.

"I'll do my very best." Lydia smiled and looked back at her mother. She remembered the day her mother had tasted the apple tarts, the day Lydia had given her desire to please over to the Lord. She had truly set her need to please her mother at the feet of Jesus, and He blessed her with a moment of maternal acceptance. *Oh, Jesus, You are too good to me.*

fifteen

Lydia jumped at the sound of knocking on her front door. George practically soared off the bed, barking and growling at the noise. Lydia rubbed her eyes, trying to force them open. She strained to see the alarm clock. "Five thirty?"

She pushed the covers off as the knocks, followed by George's intertwining of barks and growls, ensued again. Grabbing her robe, she mumbled, "Who in the world would be beating down my door at this time in the morning?"

Finally making it to the door, Lydia peered through the peephole. Lorma stood fully dressed but with her hair flowing down her back in a disheveled mess. It was the first time Lydia had seen the woman's hair down, and she would have never guessed it to be so long as to flow past her shoulders. Well, it didn't exactly flow; it kind of gathered past her shoulders.

When Lorma knocked on the door again, Lydia jumped back, clearing her mind of thoughts of Lorma's hair. She opened the door, noting the distraught expression on Lorma's face. Lydia frowned. "Lorma, what's wrong?"

The older woman pushed her way through the door and started pacing in Lydia's living room. "I don't know what to do."

Fear filled Lydia's heart. Had something happened to Gideon? Starting to fully wake up, Lydia realized something terrible must have happened for Lorma to come over this early in the morning. "Lorma, did something happen to

Gideon?" Lydia touched Lorma's arm, realizing something might be wrong with her. "Are you okay?"

Lorma sat on the couch then jumped up again. "I'm fine. Fine. You've got to go talk to Gideon."

Lydia let out a sigh of relief. Gideon must not be hurt if Lorma wanted her to talk to him. "Here now." She grabbed her friend's arm. "Let's go to the kitchen, and I'll make us some coffee. You can tell me what's going on."

Lorma shook her head but allowed Lydia to lead her. "He just can't do this. It's not what he wants." Lorma looked at Lydia. "I know my son better than he knows himself. And he hasn't really given this to God. I know." She pointed to her chest. "I can tell."

Lydia's concern and curiosity piqued. It was evident Lorma spoke of Gideon. But what decision had he made that upset his mother so much? Lydia had no idea. Gideon seemed as steady as his orchard. He was good to his family. He cared about his employee and his family. He and Lydia seemed to have some difficulty coming to terms on things, but Lydia believed that was because she cared about him in a way that wasn't reciprocated. Though she had moments of wanting to lash out at him for not caring for her, she couldn't force him to do so.

Lorma sat in a chair. She plopped her elbows on top of the table and rested her chin in her hand. "He loves you."

"What?" Lydia spun around to gawk at her older friend.

Lorma's gaze stayed trained on the table's centerpiece. She seemed to have forgotten Lydia was in the room. "Why he can't admit it to himself, I just don't know."

"What?"

"He's always been worried about doing the right thing. A

good trait. A mother can't complain about a son who wants to do what's right, but sometimes he thinks about what he thinks is the right thing instead of what God thinks is the right thing." She looked at Lydia. "Does that make sense?"

"I have no idea what you're talking about."

"Okay, one time when he was a boy he found a small kitten along the side of the road. Something or someone had abused the animal. Gideon brought the kitty home and hid her in his room to nurse her back to health." Lorma flailed her hand through the air. "Sounds like a sweet thing to do. Except Dalton is desperately allergic to cats. The poor boy blew up like a balloon. We had to rush him to the hospital, but I had no idea what had caused Dalton's reaction. I worried over foods and laundry detergents. Later that day, Sabrina found the kitten beneath Gideon's bed. Of course, we had to give the kitty to a family who could nurse her back to health. Do you see what I mean?"

Lydia furrowed her brows as she scooped coffee grounds into the coffee filter. "I still have no idea what you're talking about, Lorma."

Lorma sighed and crossed her arms in front of her chest. "Gideon actually hurt his brother by trying to help the kitten. Helping the kitten was a noble thing, but not in the way Gideon went about it. He should have helped the kitten by taking her to another house. She was adopted by our friends and led a great kitty life."

Lydia rubbed her temples. Maybe she wasn't fully awake yet, but she still had no idea what her friend was getting at. She turned on the coffeepot. *Maybe once I get a little caffeine in me, Lorma will make more sense.*

Lorma stood and walked over to the cabinets. She pulled

out two coffee mugs and set them on the counter. Touching Lydia's hand, she let out a long breath. "He loves you."

Lydia pulled her hand away and rubbed her eyes again. "Lorma, what are you talking about?"

"Gideon." The older woman smacked her hand against the counter. "What do you think I've been talking about?"

Lydia bit the inside of her lip. She tried to recall all the things Lorma had said since she walked through the door. Her friend needed to give Lydia a break. It wasn't even six yet; it was still dark outside. What did kittens and Gideon and Dalton have to do with loving her? And why would Lorma feel the need to traipse to her house in the wee hours of the morning all upset about it? "Okay. Maybe it's because I just woke up." She didn't mention that Lorma's incessant knocks had been the cause of the rude awakening. "But I have no idea what you're talking about."

"Gideon loves you."

Lydia stepped back. She swallowed the hope, excitement, denial, and disbelief that swirled within her. The softness of his kiss sprang to her mind, and she touched her lips. "No, he doesn't."

Lorma nodded. "Yes, he does."

"But he's even said—"

"He said he didn't love you?"

"In so many words, he said—"

"That's because he thinks he's supposed to marry Maria."

"What?"

Lorma poured herself a cup of coffee and made her way back over to the table. She slowly sat down. "Jim had been putting pressure on Gideon about Maria ever since her husband died, leaving her to raise the boys alone. Lately,

Maria's added to that pressure, and with Jim dying. . ."

Lydia gasped. "Jim died?"

A tear slipped down Lorma's cheek. "Yes. Four days ago. The funeral was yesterday. It was so hard. Those boys. . . Maria was beside herself." She peered at Lydia. "I tried to call. I couldn't get in touch with you."

"I was at my mom's house. She had some business for me."

Lorma nodded. "I feel so bad for Maria." She placed her hand on her chest, and her voice caught. "I know how hard it is to lose someone, but that poor girl has lost her husband and now her father in just over a year."

Lydia sat across from Lorma. She placed her hand over her friend's. "Is there anything I can do to help?"

"That's sweet of you, dear, but right now everything is fine. I'll be watching the boys since Jim helped pay her childcare expenses. I kept them yesterday so that Maria could take care of some things. I'll be feeding them, but Gideon. . ." She swiped the tear from her eye. "He's planning to ask Maria to marry him."

"He is?" Sadness wrapped around Lydia's heart so tight she feared she would suffocate.

"He thinks it's the right thing to do." She shook her head. "But you don't marry someone because you feel sorry for her or just because you want to help her. God is the ultimate Provider."

Lydia searched her mind for something to say. She hurt to the depths of her core, but maybe Gideon knew best. "Well, maybe—"

"And you definitely don't marry someone when you love someone else." Lorma's intense gaze sent shivers down Lydia's spine.

"I don't believe he loves me."

"He does. He just won't admit it."

Lydia was baffled. What could she say to Lorma? She stood and walked to the coffeepot. Warm steam tickled her nose as she poured herself a cup. She believed the older woman knew Gideon better than most mothers knew their sons, but Lydia couldn't help but feel Lorma was wrong on this. Outside of their kiss, Gideon had never openly encouraged her to believe he had feelings for her. *And even that he dismissed.*

"You have to tell him you love him, too."

Lydia almost spilled the hot coffee down her shirt. She set the pot down and gawked at Lorma. "What?"

"Tell him you love him, Lydia. Force him to see he's making a mistake."

"I will not tell him—"

"You don't love him?"

The intensity in Lorma's eyes made Lydia's knees shake. She'd been trying to suppress her growing affection for Gideon for several weeks now. Yes, she'd had a bout of overwhelming sadness at his rejection. And maybe she had believed she might love him. But he didn't return the feelings, so she'd put her full effort into the coffee shop. "Well, I—"

"You love him." Lorma laid her cup on the table with a thud. "It's okay to admit it. I know you feel vulnerable, but I promise he does love you."

"Now, Lorma—"

"Lydia, you have to stop him from doing this. Maria is in the midst of sadness. She thinks Gideon will solve her problems, but God is the only one who can do that. And Gideon doesn't love her in that way. This isn't right for either one of them."

Lydia placed both hands on her hips and faced her older friend. "I will not tell Gideon I love him, like him, or can't stand the sight of him. He's a grown man, and if he chooses to marry Maria, that is his business."

Lydia coughed back the welling of emotion that filled her throat after the outburst. *God, You have to take away these feelings I have for Gideon. I can't feel this way about a man who is marrying someone else.*

৯

Gideon scratched the several days' worth of growth on his chin. Mama had been on him several times to shave his face, but he just hadn't felt like it. His heart hurt at the loss of his employee. He knew Jim was in heaven, but that didn't stop the sadness at losing his friend. It had brought back memories of his pa, as well. Good memories and sad ones.

Having the boys around the house the day before had placed additional strain on him. He enjoyed that they kept him busy—less time to think—but it felt uncomfortable for them to be there. More pressure. *It won't feel that way once I marry Maria.*

At the moment, everything was quiet. Even Mama hadn't awoken. He glanced at his watch. It was almost seven. Mama usually arose well before this time, but Gideon figured she was overly tired from all that had happened. He leaned over in his chair and scooped up the weekly newspaper. Normally he read it right away, but with all the happenings of late, he hadn't looked at in two days. He skimmed the first few pages. An advertisement caught his eye. Lydia's coffee shop opened in less than a week.

He rested his head back against the chair and closed his eyes, allowing a vision of her to filter into his mind. Her curly, reddish hair fell around her shoulders and framed her face. Joyous twinkles filled her eyes. And those cute freckles splattered along her nose. How would he ever erase them from his thoughts?

"Hey, Gideon."

Gideon opened his eyes and leaned forward at the sound of Kelbe's voice. Heat warmed Gideon's face. He felt guilty thinking of Lydia when he should be focused on Maria and the boys. "Hey, buddy. When did you get here?"

"Just a minute ago."

"Where's your mom?"

"Looking for Lorma. Will you fix me some cereal?"

"Of course." Gideon stood and walked the little guy into the kitchen. *I hope Mama feels all right. She never sleeps this late.* He helped Kelbe onto the chair then grabbed several boxes from the cabinet. "Which one do you want?"

Kelbe pointed to the one Gideon felt sure contained enough sugar to supply a candy factory. Gideon shrugged. Either his mother or Maria had bought the cereal, so it must not have been too bad for the boy. Although, that might explain why the boys ran around with more energy than he could ever conjure for the greatest part of each day.

Gideon poured the cereal into the bowl. He opened the refrigerator, scooping out the gallon of milk. Even their fridge had blossomed with character-covered treats that he'd had no idea existed. *I'm going to have to learn about these things quick if I'm going to marry Maria.*

He frowned. Every time he thought of marrying Maria, an overwhelming sadness sank into his gut. He didn't want to dread what was right to do. Surely God would take away these feelings. He'd been praying for God to show him whom to choose—Lydia or Maria—when he received word of Jim's death. If that wasn't a sign from God, Gideon didn't know what one was.

Uneasiness wrapped itself around him. *When was the last time I spent time in God's Word?* He shook his head. Where had that come from? He'd been to church just last week. He'd been praying and seeking. God had been quiet, but it wasn't because Gideon didn't want to be in God's will.

Dread weighed him again. Something wasn't right. He still didn't have any peace about anything.

"Thanks, Gideon."

Gideon turned at the sound of Maria's voice. He wished he would feel some attraction to her, but nothing came. "No problem."

Maria smoothed the front of her pants. "Do you know where your mom went?"

"She's not here?"

Maria shook her head.

Gideon peered outside the window. "Her car's gone." He'd never even considered that she would have gone somewhere this early in the morning.

That wasn't like her. It especially wasn't like her not to leave a note or call him to let him know where she'd gone. He grabbed his keys off the rack. "I'll be back in a little bit."

I'll start with Lydia's. After turning on the ignition, Gideon shifted into drive. Within moments, he spotted Mama's car in Lydia's driveway. Relief washed over him as he pulled his vehicle in beside hers.

After jumping out of the cab, he walked up the sidewalk to Lydia's front door. He noticed she'd weeded her flowers again and that all signs of George's early-in-the-season diggings were long gone. Knocking on the door, he bit his lip. He hadn't planned to see Lydia again for a while. He figured the more distance he put between them, the quicker his heart could get over

Lydia opened the door. Concern and something else crossed her features before she lifted her lips in a tentative smile. "Hi, Gideon."

He pointed to his mother's car. "Mama's here?"

"Yes." She hesitated then opened the door more. "Come on in."

He heard shuffling in the kitchen and walked toward the noise. Spying his mother at the sink, he scratched his unshaven jaw. "Mama, what are you doing?"

"Cleaning up these breakfast dishes. What does it look like?"

"No, I mean, why are you here so early in the morning?"

"What does it matter? You won't listen to me. She won't listen to me either." She pointed to Lydia, and Lydia shrugged, lifting her hands in surrender.

"What are you talking about?" He walked over to her and touched her arm. "You're probably tired from keeping up with those boys yesterday. How long have you been up?"

"I'm fine." She shook his hand off. "Lydia is every bit as thickheaded as you. You talking about marrying people you don't—"

Gideon sucked in his breath as if she'd punched him in the gut. Surely she had not told Lydia of his plan to ask Maria to marry him. No, his mother would never do that to him. He watched as she fussed with the towel and the bowl in her hand. *Oh yes, she would.* He leaned close to her and whispered, "Mama, you did not tell Lydia about me and Maria."

"Yes, I did." She wiped her hands on a dishrag. After grabbing her purse, she stomped toward the front door. "You're both ridiculous."

Shocked, Gideon could do nothing more than watch his mother slam the door behind her. What had she said? What did Lydia think? His gaze found Lydia standing in the door leading to her soon-to-be coffee shop. She seemed as unable to move as Gideon.

Embarrassed, Gideon cleared his throat. He shoved his hands deep into his pockets. "Well, I guess I'd better go."

He moved toward the door. Lydia must still have been shocked, because she hadn't uttered a word and he hadn't heard any movement behind him. He walked out, making his way toward his truck. Things Mama may have said to her shot at him from every angle. The woman was often too opinionated and entirely too forward with her thoughts, which only surmounted his fear.

"Gideon."

Gideon turned around to find Lydia standing in the doorway. She sported a mess of disheveled hair framing her face, sleepy eyes, and an oversized robe. Lydia drew him in with intensity. "Yeah?"

"You're. . .a good man."

Gideon nodded, hopped into his truck, and drove off. What had she meant by that? Was she giving her permission for him to marry Maria? Maybe she was telling him it was the right thing to do. Whatever she meant, he felt anything but good right now.

sixteen

Lydia straightened the hem of her skirt. She hadn't bitten her nails since she was thirteen, but she found herself fighting off the urge every few seconds. The OPEN sign turned toward the public in the front door signified the beginning of her business.

She scanned the coffee shop again. A sofa, two wingback chairs, and several tables rested graciously in various places in the room. The rich color on the walls beckoned serenity. The robust scent of coffee muted the many flavors of tea she had ready for customers to choose from. Today, she'd serve both of her specialties—apple tarts and apple pies.

Looking down at her watch, she let out a slow breath to calm her anxious heart. She'd been open for two minutes. She frowned. "I wonder where Lorma is." Her friend had been just as excited, if not more so, about opening the shop. She'd promised to be here before the first customer. Lydia shrugged. "Well, there aren't any customers yet."

An immediate queasiness forced her to the nearest chair. What if no one showed up? She'd spent a good chunk of her savings and inheritance to open the place. Her mother had bought out her aunt's share of the house. For the first time in Lydia's life, her mom believed in something Lydia had chosen. What if she flopped. . .again?

Nausea overwhelmed her and she dashed into the kitchen for a lemon-lime soda, a ginger ale, anything that would keep her from hurling on her opening day. *Please God, not man.* The meaning of the Galatians and Thessalonians scriptures she'd read over and over the past few months flew into her mind.

She popped open her soda and took a slow sip. Scrutinizing the can, she said, "Please God, not man." She stood again. "Please God, not man." Lifting her face to the ceiling, she closed her eyes. "Oh, Jesus, I need only to please You. If this flops, then I will know You have something better for me."

Walking back into her coffee shop, contentment washed over her. The last few months had been some of the most trying of her life, and still her future appeared as uncertain as ever. She didn't know if this business would make it, and she'd invested so much into it. She still had deep affection for a man who didn't share her feelings. *Oh, who am I kidding? I know I love Gideon.* Her dog still chewed up things he shouldn't. Her mom would probably be livid if the business didn't thrive. And yet Lydia felt an inner peace. One that went deeper than the jitters she felt at her opening day.

A smile twitched her lips as she poured herself a large mug of coffee. *With God leading my life, nothing can shake me.*

❧

Gideon picked up a broken twig off the ground. He snapped it between his fingers. He'd grown tired of playing games. He knew what he should do, what was right. Gideon just hadn't been able to do it. Well, enough was enough.

He stomped toward the house. Maria had spent the whole day with his mother. *Just go in there and spit it out. Once I've said it, I'll feel better.* After pushing the door open, he barreled down the hall, practically running over Maria as she stepped out of the restroom. "I'm sorry." He grabbed her elbow. "Are you okay?"

She gathered her footing and looked up at him. A shy smile split her lips.

Gideon frowned. The woman appeared almost timid. He hadn't seen that side of her in a while. When she first moved here after her husband's death, she'd been sad and shy, like a wounded puppy. Once Lydia moved to town, her demeanor had changed to aggressive and flirtatious. Since her father died, Maria had been determined but sad all over again. Gideon wasn't sure who Maria really was as a person. He figured she probably wasn't sure herself after all the loss she'd had in such a short time.

"I need to talk to you." Gideon spit the words out with more force than he'd intended.

"Good. I need to talk to you, too. You first." She pushed a strand of dark hair behind her ear, and Gideon wished the motion stirred him as it did when he saw Lydia do it. But he felt nothing, and the admission of it weighed his heart.

"Well. . ." He cleared his throat, willing his mouth to utter the words his heart denied. It seemed wrong, so very wrong to issue the words he sought for this woman. But feelings could be deceiving, and he needed to focus on what was right. "I wanted. . ."

Maria's brows furrowed, and she nodded. "Go ahead."

A cold sweat washed over his body. He leaned against the wall as dizziness swept through him with such force he feared landing prone on the carpet at any moment. *Just spit it out.* "I think we should get married."

Maria's eyes widened, and her jaw dropped.

Gideon closed his eyes, allowing his head to thump against the wall. *Very romantic, Andrews. Way to draw the woman in, make her feel wanted.* He gathered his courage and looked at her again. "What I meant to say—"

Maria lifted her hand to stop him. She pursed her lips then let out a sigh. Her gaze drifted to her fingertips as she mumbled, "I thought you'd never ask."

Horror gripped Gideon's heart as his question forced him into realization that he could never love Maria as he did Lydia. *What am I doing? Oh, God, You have to see me through this.*

A vision of his wedding day passed through his mind. His bride waltzed down the aisle toward him. Lydia looked beautiful. . .

He shook his head. *Maria. I must focus on Maria.*

Maria blew out a long breath, rubbed her hands together, then intertwined her fingers. "I've been waiting to hear you say that for several months now."

He forced a smile to his lips. "Good. I haven't bought you a ring. I'll let you pick one out. When shall we set the date?"

"Do you love me?"

"Well, I. . .I mean, I. . ."

"You don't." Maria touched his arm. "And it's okay." She raked her fingers through her hair. "I thought I loved you. Thought you'd be the best thing for me and the boys. But when I saw you with Lydia. . .well, I don't want to be second place."

Shame washed over him. Mama had said the same thing on multiple occasions, but he had ignored her. "Maria, I. . ."

"The boys and I are moving to California."

"What?"

"I have two aunts who live there. My mother's sisters. They've agreed to let the boys and me move in with them until I can find a job and settle in."

"But, but. . ." Gideon shifted his weight from one foot to the other. "You don't have to leave. You. . .you and the boys love it here. I could help—"

"You're a good man, Gideon, and I appreciate all you've done for my dad, my boys, and me. I know you would help." Maria rubbed the front of her forehead. "But we've gone from Wisconsin to Indiana. We can learn to love California, too."

Determination welled within Gideon. He thought of the pain her boys would feel at having to be uprooted once again. They were too young to have to deal with such instability. It wasn't right. He stuck out his chin. "My offer stands."

Maria let out a soft laugh. "You big oaf. A month ago, maybe even a week ago, I'd have taken you up on that."

"Well, then what's the problem?"

She gazed into his eyes. "You love someone else."

"Now, I never said—"

"You never said it, but"—she placed one hand on her hip and squinted her eyes at him—"it's true just the same." She smacked her hand on her thigh. "I've already told you once. I don't want to be second place. I won't do it. I know you love my boys, and I know you like me all right, but I need a man who longs for me while he's at work or when he's away. Do you long for me like that, Gideon?"

"Well, I could—"

She flailed her hand in the air. "Listen. You need to spend some time with your Maker. I know He's been doing a work on my stubborn head for several days now. Going to California is the right thing for me and my boys." She blew out a breath. "Look, I know you're a good man who wants to do what's right. Let God show you what's right." She pointed to his chest. "For you—Gideon Andrews."

Gideon watched as she turned back, headed toward the bathroom, and shut the door. She was the second woman in the last week to tell him he was a good man. Yet, both times he'd felt anything but good.

He walked into his bedroom and grabbed his Bible off the nightstand. "You and I are going to have a good talk." He looked out his window and toward his favorite spot just inside the orchard. "And this time I'm going to do a lot of listening."

ðŸ‚

Lydia smacked her alarm clock to stop its incessant buzzing. With extreme effort, she pulled back her covers and lifted herself from the bed. Her coffee shop had been open a week, and she'd had four customers. Four.

She rubbed her eyes and rolled her head around to stretch her neck. It proved hard to wake up so early, knowing that probably no one would show. She padded into the bathroom and started the shower. *God, is there anything else I should be doing to get the word out about the shop? What should I change?*

Maybe it just wasn't meant to be. Gideon had warned her about the location. He had been concerned if there was a market for such a place in their small community. She and Lorma had shrugged him off, believing Lydia's place would be unique. Even though he'd been more than hesitant about her business, Lydia couldn't deny he'd been a constant help in getting it running.

Stepping into the shower, she closed her eyes under the warm splattering of water. Oh, how she missed that man. By now, he'd probably already proposed to Maria. She really needed to stop thinking about him. But it seemed the less she saw of him the more she longed to see him again. She let out a sarcastic breath. "I guess it's true what they say, absence does make the heart grow fonder."

She shook her head. *Think about getting the shop ready today.* "Okay. I need to make another batch of apple tarts." She snarled. She and Lorma had eaten most of the first batch. She grimaced when she thought of her friend. Lorma had been just as disappointed as Lydia at the lack of customers. The four people who'd come had been friends of Lorma's from the church. One of the ladies didn't even purchase anything, just stopped by to say hello.

After finishing her shower, she blow-dried her hair, allowing the curls to lie naturally around her shoulders. She scooped her devotional and Bible into her hands and made her way to the kitchen table. Over the last few months, she'd grown accustomed to spending her quiet time gazing out at Grandma's beautiful backyard.

God, I need to know You're still in control and that I am living surrendered to You. She opened her devotional and read a scripture from the book of Philippians. Allowing the words to seep thoroughly into her heart, she gazed at the seemingly never-ending sea of foliage. "God, I choose not to worry. I will pray and petition You that I may know Your will and have perfect peace."

Feeling refreshed, she walked over to the kitchen counter. She gathered the ingredients she'd need for the tarts. George trotted beside her, wagging his tail. She looked down at him. "You know what, George, I have no idea what God has planned." George barked and lifted his nose high in the air. "I'll just keep doing what I'm doing, fully surrendered to Him. He'll show me."

The doorbell rang, and George lit into a chorus of yelps. *I really should have trained that dog a few things more than just to where to use the bathroom.* Lydia glanced at her watch. It was way too early for a customer. Even Lorma wouldn't come over this early. She huffed. *Unless she's trying to get me to profess all my feelings to Gideon.* The doorbell rang again. "I'm coming."

ᘉ

Gideon almost turned around and headed home when he heard Lydia's voice from inside the house. He could hear the tapping of her feet as she approached. Part of him wanted to run. What would she say when he told her how he felt? After all, they'd only known each other for two months. But the other part of him wanted to scoop her into his arms the moment she opened that door.

The door opened and the latter desire took over. Before he had time to even think about it, Gideon bent over and grabbed Lydia into his arms. She gasped, and he realized he hadn't given her time to even know who he was. "It's okay, Lydia. It's me." He held her tight, relishing her lithe form and how well she fit in his arms.

"Gideon, put me down." Her tone did not belie the excitement he felt, and though he complied with her request, he took his own time in placing her back on her feet. "What are you doing?" She smacked at his arms. She could haul off and duke him in the face. He deserved it. He'd been a fool, and he could hardly contain himself with the freedom and the joy he felt. If Lydia didn't return his feelings—and he prayed, oh, how he prayed she did—he'd have to spend every waking moment he could sitting at her house, drinking her coffee or tea or whatever she made, and wooing her until she decided she'd couldn't resist marrying him.

"Lydia, I've spent a lot of time with God the last few days."

She crossed her arms and rubbed her triceps with her hands. "Okay, so?"

"So I came upon this scripture in Galatians." He scratched his weeklong beard. *Ugh. I could have cleaned up a little bit for her.* He put his hand down. He didn't need to worry about things like that at this moment. This moment was meant for convincing Lydia. "I believe God's been trying to speak this truth to me all summer, but I didn't listen."

She furrowed her eyebrows and took a step back.

He grabbed her hand and pulled her onto the porch with him. "There's a verse that says, 'Am I now trying to win the approval of men, or of God? Or am I trying to please men? If I were still trying to please men, I would not be a servant of Christ.'"

She gasped. Pulling her hand away, she lifted her eyebrows and nodded her head, but her expression displayed something. Maybe it was only that she thought he'd lost his mind. And in truth, he had. He'd lost *his* mind and gained God's. Somehow, he had to tell Lydia all the amazing things God had been showing him over the last week.

"Galatians 1, verse 10?"

"Yes! That's the verse." Elation filled his lungs. "You know it, too." *God, have You already prepared her heart? Oh, how I pray You have.*

Her gaze lifted past him and up to the heavens. "Yes, I know the verse. I memorized it and one from Thessalonians, too."

"Then you already know what I've struggled with. I spent the whole summer trying to convince myself that I could fall in love with Maria because she needed stability, and she and Jim were convinced I was that stability. I even told her we should get married..."

Lydia's gaze flew back to his. Emotion flicked through her eyes before she squinted at him. "You knocked on my door at"—Lydia looked at her watch—"six in the morning to tell me you're marrying Maria?"

"No." Gideon had to hold back the laughter that wanted to burst from within. "I'm not marrying Maria. I want to marry you."

She gasped and lifted her hand to her mouth.

The love he felt poured through his veins as he watched the pure and innocent surprise that filled her eyes. "I love you, Lydia. I've loved you all summer, probably since the first moment I met you when George ruined my first batch of peaches." Gideon glanced through the glass door and noticed the overgrown pup wag his tail, anxious to join them.

"But?"

Gideon looked back at Lydia. Her eyes brimmed with tears as she shook her head. Fearing she would reject him, Gideon grabbed her hands again. "I've spent this whole summer running from my feelings for you. I thought I was supposed to marry Maria because it was the right, the noble thing to do." With one hand, he brushed a strand of her hair, softer than he'd imagined, behind her ear. "I tried to fight off my love for you, but God wouldn't let it go. You're the one He's chosen for me."

Pulling her hands away, she swiped her eyes. "Well, I don't know what to say."

"Say you love me."

She bit her bottom lip, and Gideon thought the heavens would burst from the silence. Even the insects seemed to await her answer. A slow smile bowed her lips. "I do love you, Gideon."

Happiness welled within him as he took the antique ring he'd purchased the day before from his pants pocket. He got down on one knee and held out the elegant white-gold band with a circular diamond wrapped in a square setting and joined on each side by two smaller diamonds. "Say you'll marry me."

"I will."

seventeen

"Why are you getting married so fast?"

Gideon stopped adjusting his tie and looked at his older brother, Dalton. "I love her, and after all we've been through this past summer, I'm positive she's the one God designed for me."

"But we've only had a chance to meet her a couple times," Cameron joined in. "Caitlyn and I have dated twice as long as you, and we aren't getting married until spring."

Gideon laughed. "Well, I couldn't let my little brother tie the knot before me." Glancing out his bedroom window, he noted the fullness of his apple orchard. The tall trees bragged of lush green, orange, yellow, and pink leaves and full, ripened apples. Already, he'd had several school and church groups enjoy his land. He had never been so excited or thankful when Lydia insisted they marry in front of the land God had given him. "Besides, Indiana is beautiful in October."

Dalton raised his eyebrows and nodded. "Can't argue with that."

Gideon straightened the front of his black tuxedo jacket. "I'm going to find the girls."

"They'll never let you see Lydia," Cameron resounded.

"They have to at least let me talk to her."

Before his brothers could protest, Gideon walked out of the room. Making his way down the hall, he knew his slew of sisters had Lydia in one of the many rooms jam-packed with giggling women. Figuring out which one would be the test. He knocked on the closest door. "Lydia?"

"Gideon, she's not in here." Natalie's voice sounded through the door. "And if she were, I wouldn't let her see you anyway. Grooms can't see the bride before the wedding."

"I just want to talk to her," Gideon growled. He didn't care about that silly tradition. Between a rehearsal and bridal parties, or whatever they called them, Gideon had hardly had the chance to see Lydia alone over the last few weeks. He missed her something terrible and simply wanted to hear her voice before they stood before all those people. *If I get a peek at her and maybe a little kiss, that would be all right, too.*

Gideon knocked on the next door. "Lydia?"

"Gideon Andrews," Lydia's mother's voice boomed from inside the room, "what are you doing? It's bad luck to see the bride before the wedding."

"It's okay, Mom," Lydia's soft voice echoed. "I don't believe in luck." She sounded nervous.

Does she think we've moved too fast, Lord? We could have waited. It's just that I know she's the right one, and I've wanted so much to make her mine in name as well as in my heart.

The door opened just a crack. All he could see were mounds and mounds of white material and Lydia's exquisite face. She smiled when their eyes met, and a slight blush reddened her cheeks.

Her voice came out just louder than a whisper. "Hey."

"Are you nervous?"

"A little. What about you?"

"I can hardly wait to make you my wife." He caressed her cheek, and she closed her eyes at his touch. "You seem nervous. Did we move too fast?"

"Oh no." She nestled her cheek into his hand. "I'm just ready to say our vows and see you again. Just you and me."

Anticipation filled his heart. He longed for time with her. Just her. As much as he couldn't wait to see his bride adorned in a beautiful dress and walking down the aisle toward him, he yearned even more for time alone with her.

"Lydia," Rita's voice boomed, "shut that door."

"My mom's making me nervous." Her eyes twinkled. "I guess that's her job today."

Gideon looked at his watch. "Half an hour and you'll be Mrs. Gideon Andrews."

"I can hardly wait."

❧

Lydia placed her hand in the crook of her mother's arm. A moment of wishing she'd been closer to her father washed over her, but he had died from cancer a few years after he and her mom divorced. He'd never really had much to do with his family before that, either.

She peeked at her mother, whose eyes brimmed with tears. Her mom had done the best job she knew how. Allison had always been more like Mom, making Lydia feel like a misfit, but Lydia knew deep down her mother loved her. Over the last few months, since she and Gideon became engaged, she'd even noted hints that her mother had grown interested in learning more about God. The thought sent shivers of excitement through her.

"You ready?" Lydia whispered.

"To give away my baby?" Rita's voice caught. "Not really."

Lydia squeezed her mother's arm. "I love you, Mom."

"I. . .love you, too," her mother said as "The Wedding March" started.

Lydia allowed her mother's words to sink into her heart. Her mother loved her. It may have been the first time in her life Lydia had ever heard those words from her lips.

Amazingly, it didn't matter.

Sure, she thanked God for the relationship that was just beginning to blossom with her mom. One in which Lydia honored her mother's thoughts and suggestions. One in which Rita cared about and loved Lydia. She wanted to share fears, frustrations, disappointments, and joys with her mom. But Lydia's confidence, her confirmation of who she was as a person, came solely from God. Lydia inhaled at the truth of it. Her greatest desire remained to please her Abba, her Daddy God.

Partially hidden behind a tree, the twosome stepped out and Lydia gazed down the nature's rug that served as her white carpet. Looking beyond Gideon, the preacher, and their various attendants, she took in the mixture of deep green, pink, yellow, orange, and red colors of the leaves. She couldn't have put a more beautiful arrangement together if she'd spent thousands of dollars.

Her gaze skimmed the audience filled with friends and family. Pride, pure and innocent, swelled within her heart as she took in Gideon's family. *I can't wait to become a member of the Andrews clan.*

Saving the best for last, she took in her soon-to-be husband. The sweet, anticipatory smile that lit his face drew her to him. Her gaze connected with his, and she couldn't let go. How she longed to be in his arms, to be his wife, until death parted them.

After what seemed an eternity, she found herself face-to-face with Gideon. The words of the minister and then her mother seemed to drift into the wind. All she could think about was the strong yet soft touch of Gideon's hand around hers; the mixture of hazel, green, and brown swimming in his eyes; and the slight stubble that was already shading his jaw. How she loved him!

Words of promise uttered from her lips. She saw Gideon's lips move and knew he repeated the vows, as well. All she could think of was the overwhelming peace she felt at becoming Gideon's wife.

For most of her life, Lydia had felt unstable and insecure. God had changed all that. Everything in her life had changed when she met Him. She still had a lot of growing to do, but she'd grown a lot over the last few months, as well.

"By the power vested in me"—the preacher's words penetrated her thoughts, and she lifted her eyebrows to see Gideon's smile deepen and a mischievous gleam fill his eyes—"I now pronounce you man and wife. You may kiss your bride."

Gideon wrapped his arms around her. The warmth and strength of his embrace nearly took her breath. His lips met hers, and she allowed herself the bliss that swept through her. She'd never felt such happiness. But it was the peace—the amazing, everlasting peace—that filled, and would always sustain, her heart.

epilogue

Twenty-one months later

Lydia closed the door to the house that once belonged to her grandmother. It belonged to Lorma now. Soon, it would be home to Cameron and his new bride, Caitlyn, as well. Gideon had never replaced Jim as an employee after his death. The upkeep of the orchard had become more than Gideon could bear alone, and when his brother offered to help, Gideon had jumped at the chance. Lydia could hardly wait to get to know her sister-in-law better.

After setting the basket of baked goodies and coffee on the ground, Lydia opened the back door of the car. She wiped the sweat from her brow. *Whew, it is hot.* Gideon's—no *their*—family would be arriving any minute for the annual Independence Day celebration. Lorma had most of the food prepared at Lydia and Gideon's house. Lydia had simply run over to what was once her coffee shop for a few after-dinner-and-fireworks treats.

The coffee shop, as a business, had closed a little over a year before. Though he'd been supportive to the end, Gideon had been right that people simply didn't travel out of their way to visit the place. At first, Lydia hurt at the admission of defeat, feeling she'd misheard God's direction. But when different churches, school clubs, and other groups requested gatherings at her shop for various Bible studies, meetings, and other activities,

Lydia realized the shop had been formed for a reason, not for business but for ministry.

Now that Lorma, with the aid of her daughter, Kylie, and son-in-law, Ryan, had purchased the house from Lydia's mother, Lorma had taken over the bulk of the ministry. She thrived among the company that frequented her house. Lydia had never seen her mother-in-law so happy.

Lydia placed one hand in the small of her back and stretched out the slight ache she'd had most of the day. Rubbing her protruding belly with the other, Lydia smiled. With their babies due in just under a month, she was thankful Lorma had taken over the ministry. Lydia would have her hands full for a while.

Lydia jumped when her cell phone vibrated in her front pocket. She pulled it out and read Gideon's name on the screen. Actually, she read the nickname he'd typed into her phone for himself—My Hero. She giggled as she pushed the TALK button. "Yes, My Hero?"

"That's right, and I always will be." His voice sounded husky and possessive. "Are you okay? I was starting to get worried."

She loved how protective he'd become of her since they'd discovered they'd be parents. "I've only been gone thirty minutes, but I'm coming home right now."

"You've got five minutes."

"Yes, sir." She couldn't stop the salute of her free hand.

"I love you, Private."

"I love you, too, Drill Sergeant."

Lydia laughed as she closed her cell phone. Gideon's protectiveness grew when they discovered she carried twins, so she'd taken to calling him the military name. Fine with the nickname, he'd given her one, as well. Though at times he smothered her with his concern, she knew it was out of love. She relished that he cared for her and their babies so much.

After placing the basket in the backseat, she made her way around the car and got in. A slight tightening surrounded her stomach, and she let out a long breath. She'd had Braxton Hicks contractions for well over a month. The doctor had told her they were common and nothing to worry about, but as the babies got bigger, the contractions had grown stronger.

She started the car and within moments arrived at her home. She noticed Sabrina's and Kylie's vans in the driveway. The two were usually the first to arrive at their family gatherings, and Lydia could hardly wait to see them.

Gideon met her outside and opened the door. His smile turned to a frown. "Are you okay? You look flushed."

She laughed. "I'm fine. I just get tired quickly these days. Why don't you carry the basket inside for me?"

"Of course." Gideon opened the back door and hefted the basket without problem.

Before they could make it into the house, Chloe and Trevor pulled into the drive. Lydia clapped her hands. They hadn't seen their newest niece for a couple weeks. Lydia could hardly wait to get her hands on the toddler. "I'm going to see Faith. I'll be just a minute."

Gideon chuckled. "I believe you'll have your hands full with squirming little ones soon enough."

At his words, another dull ache draped around her midsection. She touched her belly.

Gideon touched her, as well. "Are you sure you're all right?"

She swatted her hand through the air. "Of course. I'm fine. Go help your mom."

Lydia waddled away from him and toward their newest

visitors. Already Chloe had unbuckled the toddler and lifted her onto her hip. Lydia took in Faith's full head of light brown hair. If Lydia guessed right, the girl would look just like her mom. "Gracie-girl, come here and let Aunt Lydia hold you." Faith giggled and reached for Lydia, who took the toddler from her mother.

Chloe smiled. "You'll get tired of this soon enough." She rubbed Lydia's belly then furrowed her eyebrows. "You're awfully tight."

"I've been having a lot of Braxton Hicks."

Chloe studied her a moment. "Is your back hurting?"

Lydia kissed Faith's chubby cheeks. "Just a bit." She looked up at Chloe. "But look at me. I'm huge."

The fifty pounds she'd gained in eight months had done a number on her confidence at times. The stretch marks and aches that went with the quick weight gain had only been tolerable because Gideon remained reassuring of his continued attraction to her.

Chloe took Faith from Lydia's arms and handed her to Trevor. She hooked her arm through Lydia's and guided her toward the house. "We're going to see Mama."

Another tightness overwhelmed Lydia's stomach, and she gripped Chloe's arm, releasing a long breath.

Chloe's eyebrows lifted. "It's just as I thought." She guided Lydia the rest of the way to the house. "Mama," Chloe's voice echoed through the home.

Lydia looked back to see two more of Gideon's siblings had pulled up the drive.

"Lydia's in labor."

Lydia looked back into the house. Her gaze locked with Gideon's. The look of pure terror that wrapped his face was proof enough—today, they were having their babies.

≈

Lydia opened her eyes. The labor had not gone as smoothly as she had hoped. Her body refused to progress even with the aid of a most painful medication. Soon one of the babies had gone into distress, and the doctors were forced to perform a C-section. Lydia had never seen Gideon so unglued. The nurse had given him ginger ale and crackers to keep him from passing out and being admitted himself.

Now, lying in the hospital bed, Lydia felt sore but much more at peace. The nurses had been wonderful to her and her family the two days she'd been there so far. Her gaze floated around the room until she found the figure sitting in the chair beside her. The man of her dreams held the most precious treasures she'd ever met—her sons. Lorma's brood of ten grandsons and twelve granddaughters had been made even when Lydia gave birth to two boys.

Gideon must have sensed she'd awoken as he looked up from the boys and locked gazes with her. "You are the most amazing woman in the world."

His genuine awe of her brought tears to her eyes. "We serve an amazing God who has blessed us beyond what we deserve."

"Amen to that."

"Is it time for them to nurse?" Though her stomach protested the movement, Lydia gently sat up in the bed.

"I think so." Gideon stood. "Which one first?"

"I'll take both." Lydia grinned at the look of shock on Gideon's face. "The nurse showed me how to hold them like footballs." She fluffed and situated a pillow on each side of her.

Gideon handed her one boy then the other. Within minutes,

both were nursing soundly. "I can't believe I'm a dad." He pushed a strand of hair away from her face. "I was just getting used to being a husband."

"I'm that tough, huh?"

He kissed her forehead. "I've loved every minute with you."

Tears welled in her eyes again. She'd cried more the last few days than she had in her lifetime. "I love you, Gideon." She lifted her face to accept a kiss on the lips. "You're a great dad."

His stomach growled as he straightened to his full height. "It's been a while since breakfast."

Lydia looked at the hospital clock below the television and gasped. "It's three o'clock. Go get some lunch."

"Will you be okay?"

She nodded. "There's a button right beside my hand I can push if I need help."

"Okay." He kissed her forehead again. "I'll be back in a minute."

She watched as her "hero," as her phone said, walked out the door. Peering down at the fuzzy-haired, healthy boys in her arms, she exhaled a long breath of contentment.

All of her life, Lydia had longed for peace. When she finally met Jesus, He'd given the fullness of His mercy and love. She finally accepted His pleasure in her, and then He blessed her with the three most adorable fellows she'd ever know.

She lifted her face toward the ceiling and closed her eyes. *Oh, Jesus, You are so good. Your delight in me is humbling, but I'll take it. Your peace is my greatest desire.*

A Letter To Our Readers

Dear Reader:

In order that we might better contribute to your reading enjoyment, we would appreciate your taking a few minutes to respond to the following questions. We welcome your comments and read each form and letter we receive. When completed, please return to the following:

Fiction Editor
Heartsong Presents
PO Box 719
Uhrichsville, Ohio 44683

1. Did you enjoy reading *In Pursuit of Peace* by Jennifer Johnson?
   ❏ Very much! I would like to see more books by this author!
   ❏ Moderately. I would have enjoyed it more if

   _____

   _____

   _____

2. Are you a member of **Heartsong Presents**? ❏ Yes ❏ No
   If no, where did you purchase this book? _____

   _____

3. How would you rate, on a scale from 1 (poor) to 5 (superior), the cover design? _____

4. On a scale from 1 (poor) to 10 (superior), please rate the following elements.

   ____ Heroine   ____ Plot
   ____ Hero   ____ Inspirational theme
   ____ Setting   ____ Secondary characters

5. These characters were special because? _____
_____
_____

6. How has this book inspired your life? _____
_____
_____

7. What settings would you like to see covered in future
   Heartsong Presents books? _____
_____
_____

8. What are some inspirational themes you would like to see
   treated in future books? _____
_____
_____

9. Would you be interested in reading other **Heartsong
   Presents** titles? ❏ Yes ❏ No

10. Please check your age range:
        ❏ Under 18   ❏ 18-24
        ❏ 25-34   ❏ 35-45
        ❏ 46-55   ❏ Over 55

Name_____
Occupation _____
Address _____
City, State, Zip_____

Along Came a Cowboy

Saddle up for a fast-paced ride. Rachel Donovan dreams of building a healing complex. The only thing standing in her way is Shady Grove's zoning laws and a bull-headed cowboy. Can Jack win Rachel's love, or will he wind up becoming the lone rancher?

Contemporary, paperback, 304 pages, 5³/₁₆" x 8"

HEARTSONG
PRESENTS

If you love Christian romance…

$10.⁹⁹

You'll love Heartsong Presents' inspiring and faith-filled romances by today's very best Christian authors…Wanda E. Brunstetter, Mary Connealy, Susan Page Davis, Cathy Marie Hake, and Joyce Livingston, to mention a few!

When you join Heartsong Presents, you'll enjoy four brand-new, mass market, 176-page books—two contemporary and two historical—that will build you up in your faith when you discover God's role in every relationship you read about!

Mass Market 176 Pages

Imagine…four new romances every four weeks—with men and women like you who long to meet the one God has chosen as the love of their lives…all for the low price of $10.99 postpaid.

To join, simply visit www.heartsong presents.com or complete the coupon below and mail it to the address provided.

- -

YES! Sign me up for Heartsong!

NEW MEMBERSHIPS WILL BE SHIPPED IMMEDIATELY!
Send no money now. We'll bill you only $10.99 postpaid with your first shipment of four books. Or for faster action, call 1-740-922-7280.

NAME _____

ADDRESS _____

CITY _____ STATE _____ ZIP _____

MAIL TO: HEARTSONG PRESENTS, P.O. Box 721, Uhrichsville, Ohio 44683
or sign up at **WWW.HEARTSONGPRESENTS.COM**